Happiness
at
Last

Vivien Ayinotu

authorHOUSE®

*AuthorHouse™ UK*
*1663 Liberty Drive*
*Bloomington, IN 47403 USA*
*www.authorhouse.co.uk*
*Phone: 0800.197.4150*

*Published by AuthorHouse 02/05/2018*

*ISBN: 978-1-5246-8165-4 (sc)*
*ISBN: 978-1-5246-8166-1 (e)*

*Print information available on the last page.*

*Any people depicted in stock imagery provided by Thinkstock are models, and such images are being used for illustrative purposes only. Certain stock imagery © Thinkstock.*

*This book is printed on acid-free paper.*

To a beautiful soul, my lovely mother
whose life has inspired me a lot.

# *One*

**Achafu** Street in Enugu city was where Ikedinachi had spent most of his childhood days and still could not disengage himself from the activities of this lovely city. The town has few parks and five popular restaurants. Among its peculiar features were how people lived in yards and related closely with one another.

Ikedinachi is the first son in a family of three; two boys and a girl. Ugonna was in class six while Adanna, the baby of the house was in elementary school.

Ikedinachi is five years older than Ugonna because his parents, Mr. and Mrs. Okoro had a difficult time having another child after his birth in 1972. He had both his primary and secondary education in public schools and had good grades in his WAEC. He admired businessmen and couldn't wait to try his luck by experimenting to see what the labour market has to offer him the moment he left school. His parents wanted him to go to the university because he was brilliant he insisted on venturing into business first and then study sometime in the future.

"Ikedinachi my son, why have you decided to make a mockery of your parents? Do you want people to laugh at us?" his mother asked him.

"We can afford to send you to a higher institution." As she talked, the tone of her voice became faint in a deep feeling of disappointment.

Ikedinachi's father sighed and said to him, "Son, we have visited this topic several times, but it looks as though I have been pouring water on stones or perhaps I have been talking to deaf ears, but, if you insist, we shall discuss later." He left Ikedinachi and his mother.

Mrs. Okoro sobbed the more as she could not ascertain whether her husband had accepted their son's wish or not. She knew her husband well and knew there was no need trying to argue with him over their son's decision as it has been troubling the family for some time. Ikedinachi loved his mother so much and could not bear to watch her cry. He held her close and promised her that he would become a graduate in future but had always had his eyes fixed on business.

Early in the morning the next day at 5 a.m., Mr. Okoro woke his son up to a father and son conversation. The talk dragged till his younger ones woke up to their chores and prepared for school.

"My son, did you say that you do not want to complete your education first before other distractions like eh… business? He quipped while nonchalantly chipping away on his chewing stick.

"Yes, papa."

"Papa, I will further my education later in the future, but I want to make some money first, and I want the best for my siblings too."

"Ewooo! Ikedi, you want to help your poor father? He interjected in mock surprise. Now, listen to me. You are all my children, and I need no help from anyone."

"Mama Ikedi, come and hear your son!" he shouted and continued without a response from his wife, not that he expected any though.

"The God that it pleased to let me have you all will give me whatever it will take to make life comfortable for each of you. Your mother and I are trying our best. There are decisions that as a child you do not make for yourself without seeking your parents' opinion because they can totally disagree with you. As your father, my primary responsibility is to raise, protect and direct you. I cannot watch you take a wrong path. Bear in mind that we your parents can never mislead you, we know what is best for you and have seen it all. And this is one of them."

He paused and continued "Business is good; you will become a businessman if that is what your heart desires, but first of all, you need to have a solid foundation in life education wise, which will also guide you even better in business. Besides, you will have to watch your mates graduate from different Universities. Is that what you wish yourself?"

"No Papa but..." Ikedinachi found his head in between his palms as he leaned backwards on the sofa.

He knew it was never going to be easy convincing his father, but did not know it would get to this extent either.

His father continued, "I know you are a good son and would love to help your parents and that is the dream of every parent; including myself- *he pointed towards his chest as he speaks* - to have reasonable kids but please I beg you in God's name, you are still a child, we are not expecting any help from you now. When that time comes, we will let you know," his father pleaded.

"We want a better future for every one of you, and none of you should be sacrificed for the other's progress rather your mother and I are here to make the sacrifices, where necessary. That is why we are your Parents."

Ikedinachi's head was filled with thoughts as his father almost brainwashed him but he didn't want to disrespect him by arguing. Besides, he did not want to be perceived as a disobedient son and had always wanted to set good example for his younger ones.

"Papa, I have heard all that you have said. I have always dreamt of becoming a businessman but if you and mama insist that I go to University first, then I will have to. At least, to make you both happy and proud parents."

"I am glad you have reasoned with your father. I want you to bear in mind that apart from making us happy and proud, it is primarily for your own good. Do not worry, you will find out in time. We are proud of you, son."

"Now I must leave you so that I won't be late for work."

"Nkem, your water will soon be cold, I hope you know what the time is?" Mrs. Okoro called out having kept for her husband warm water for bathing some minutes ago.

"I will be there in seconds Obidiya."

He hurriedly had his bath, had breakfast of tea and bread with akara balls and left for work. Mr. Okoro is a civil servant and is always at work before time, he was known for that. Despite the hurry, he was able to tell his wife that he succeeded in convincing their son about going to the University. On hearing that, Mrs. Okoro giggled silently as she did not want her son to know what had transpired. She likes sitting beside her husband when he eats, even when she doesn't want to have an early morning meal. As a trader, she wakes up early to go about her morning duties before heading to the market. In the past, she sold her goods; farm produce of all sorts which are highly dependent on the season as majority of the items were seasonal- in a shop she jointly owned with a friend. However, in the last five years, she had been able to get her own shop with the help of her husband.

Meanwhile, Ikedinachi remained calm all through the day which crept into subsequent days. Gradually, he began to loosen up. His mother sensing his uneasiness over this period approached him to enable him voice out his feelings. Like an overfilled glass of beer, he poured out his heart to her and narrated how he had imagined things to be in his life and how following the persistent persuasion from them and the last chat with his father, he was left with no choice than to succumb to their dance-tune. He sounded more like a powerless chicken that has succumbed to its fate.

"I am your mother," Mrs. Okoro pointed towards her chest, "all we want is the best for you, Ikem." Ikem is his pet-given name by his mother. "We both love you and will always be there to guide you. I understand how you feel, my son." She hugged and held him close to her chest and reassured him.

Ikedinachi had the whole day to himself and could not help the bursts of ideas in his head. He thought of how he would break the news to his peers that he will no longer go into business as he has always boasted, it made him feel bad. His desire to start rolling in cash in no distance time and being able to buy things he needed for himself, without having to ask his parents for money dashed.

Nevertheless, he recalled that other students had talked more often about going to the University. "Maybe they seem more reasonable than me, but I was brilliant in school like them as well." That flicker of thought made him realise that his parents might not be wrong after all. Besides, he might be able to focus more on studies at this tender age than when he gets older; he kept thinking as he tried to resolve issues in his head. He felt a bit better.

# Two

**At** nineteen, Ikedinachi already looked overgrown for his age. He was dark, hairy, tall -like his father, and hugely built. He expresses himself well both in his mother tongue -*igbo*- and his lingua franca - *English*. He has sideburns and likes wearing his grown naturally-carved beard which made him look more handsome and advanced in age. He was loved by all that knew him due to his charming and caring personality.

Following the conversation with his parents, he still had to convince himself that University was the best option for him now. He fought within himself and was able to bring himself to focus and study for higher institution. He made the necessary preparations and took the requisite examination for entry into the University. His parents were very supportive and wished him well.

The following couple of months were worrisome for him as he waited anxiously for the release of the lists of successful candidates. He often wondered how fast things change; barely a couple of month's back he was kicking against *any going-to-University* idea, and now he hopes to be among the successful candidates. He could not wait to be told that he made it through to the University pre-placement exam – JAMB, as it is known, partly because he took the exam and failing would not be an option but mainly to make his parents proud. They would be more excited than him, and he simply knew it.

Luck was on his side as he was successful. A colleague of his had stopped by to tell him that he saw his name on the list when he accompanied his cousin to check for his result in Enugu State University of Science and technology, popularly known as ESUT for short.

"Yes, I sat for the examination," he was breathing very fast.

"Are you serious? So, congratulation is in order? I was thinking it was a coincidence."

"Emm… what?" He asked in anxiety. He began adjusting his clothes properly and was ready to make his way to ESUT to see his name on the list with his own eyes.

"Hey! Ikedinachi, why did you have to fool others by making them think you have no interest in going to the University?" Enuma sounded very furious, not like someone who just congratulated a mate.

He continued, "I remember vividly that you talked about various business ideas most times and how prepared you were to venture into them as soon as we left school. I never imagined people could be that deceitful and I did not expect that from you. By the way, I sat for a different University, and they are yet to release their result. I was not caught in your web though."

"Oh! Enuma do not sound like that." Ikedinachi was sadened by his tone and how he has misunderstood his situation.

"It is not exactly as you have made it look. I have always said that and meant it, but my parents have never supported me, so I simply gave in to their idea. It was a difficult moment for me. I am sorry if that was how you felt then, I did not intend to discourage others from going to the University."

Enuma was not sure if he meant what he was saying. For all he cared, he had told him his piece of mind, and it was obvious that he was truly angered.

"Well, congrats again."

"Thank you," Ikedinachi replied this time. "Enuma, thanks for stopping by to let me know."

Ikedinachi hurried to the university which was less than 10km from his house to confirm the news himself. Within minutes, he was at the University. He was shaking at the sight of his name among the list of successful students. He started scribbling his admission number, his name and department on a piece of paper he had brought out from the side pocket of his trouser. Ordinarily, he would have noted only the number, but he was very nervous and copied both the number and his own name. He did not know exactly what to do, whether to tour around the school or to go home and share the news with his family and friends. It was as though that guilty version of him previously before Enuma did not exist anymore.

Eventually, he settled for going home and made his way. In the bus, there were still vacant seats, but he chose to stand and hold on to the centre rail. Fortunately, due to the traffic and busy roads, other passengers did not notice his nerves. Few minutes of traffic and numerous stops to let in passengers or to let them off prolonged his journey and he did not seem to be bothered as he daydreamed all through.

It was when a woman who was carrying a heavy load rushed into the bus and mistakenly stepped on him that he realised that he needed to move further inside the bus. The woman pushed him out of her way without blinking an eye.

"Can't you see those vacant seats?" she shouted at him as if they were quarrelling as she got herself a seat.

Reluctantly, he moved backwards and sat down. He felt relieved and realised that he was exhausted and had not eaten prior to Enuma's visit. He suddenly ran through his friend's visit in his head and sighed in relief. Within minutes, they were close to his bus stop and he alighted when they drove to the junction that led to his house.

He met Adanna and Ugonna who had come back from school and shared his latest news with them. As little as Adanna was, she was happy for him, maybe because she noticed that his brothers were both happy. He later told his parents when they got home, and they were all overjoyed to know his name was among the successful candidates.

Mrs. Okoro was the happiest of all, if it were to be judged by emotional display. Her mouth was filled with praises and prayers as she thanked God for seeing her son through and beckoning on him to perfect what he has started in his life. Usually, Adanna would join on the songs, she was familiar with the tune, including mumbling the words like they were all meaningless. However, this time she started chanting her school rhymes:

*The day is bright, is bright and fair*
*Oh, happy day, the day of joy.*
*The day is bright, is bright and fair*
*Oh, happy day, the day of joy.*
*Mama Jollof Rice!*

In her school, the song was basically for marching into the classroom but for all she cared, everyone in the house was happy and the day turned out to be bright to her, despite the time being 5.30 p.m. However, her song was not in vain because when she shouted the 'Jollof Rice' part so loud her mother told her that indeed she was going to serve rice jollof that night.

The entire family was at peace and had one of their best Christmas celebration. They all jubilated and thanked God for his favours upon them.

Having gained admission the previous year, Ikedinachi was already a first-year student in the department of banking and finance in ESUT. His parents decided that he lived in the hostel to enable him focus more on his studies and stay away from the hazards which could be encountered while going to school from home on a daily basis. Ikedinachi found their reason to be a good one as it would enable him to experience campus life. Besides, he had not lived away from home before and would love to explore what it feels like not living with his family.

Fortunately for him, a high school classmate of his, Obinna, was in the same university and department with him and that meant he already had a friend.

Obinna comes from an average family and has always been very serious with his education. He aspires to have a doctorate in the future, and those who know him well know about his passion for academic pursuit, although he seldom talks about it. He hails from Udi and lives in Echefu Street but far away from Ikedinachi's neighbourhood. He was relieved to have seen someone he already knew as it would enable him to cope better in his new environment.

"Ikedi!" he shouted.

"Obyno! Long time!" They rushed towards each other and shook hands.

"So, you are here too. I'm happy seeing someone I know. I suppose I saw your name the day I checked mine but was sure it was a coincidence because I can recall all those your 'business' chants in school. Happy to see you."

"Really? I guess I was anxious that very day that I saw my name and did not check further."

Filled with ecstasy of seeing each other, they both laughed.

"You are right. I was going to go on the business path, but my Parents would not give that a thought. So, they've won for now."

"That's great. Parents often know what's best for their children."

"Yes, Obi. I am glad to have you here too." Ikedinachi was surprised the way Obinna handled the situation in a very reasonable and mature way unlike the awkward way Enuma had approached him some weeks ago. There was much settling in that they had to do.

Campus life was very strange to them compared to their school days. Ikedinachi shares a room with three other students of different faculty. They partitioned their room into four cubicles with curtains. The curtains were specially tailored and have a long zip which can be locked for privacy and serves as a route for entrance or exit.

In most hostels in the campus as well as theirs, students cook outside their rooms. They have taps-*which are most times not functional,* and water-tanks in the building for water supply. Luckily for them, they have toilets and bathrooms on each floor of the building, and cleaners who take care of the entire vicinity.

They toured round the school and observed that the school premises was only a stone throw from the hostel area. Lecture halls were packed with long wooden seats, a sturdy built table in front of the class, presumably for the lecturer and a blackboard attached to the wall. There were old and dirty ceiling fans which hung loosely from the ceiling-*though they never fall*. Ikedinachi described most of the fans as 'automatic' when he found out that they only function whenever there is power supply and go off when power failure occurs.

They had fun while chatting and walking around the whole place. Ikedinachi didn't like being late for lectures and tried to be in the lecture hall in time to enable him to secure a better position. Most times, he sat together with his friend Obinna, though being a jovial person, he made more friends.

He found his first lectures interesting. He enjoyed interactive classes and usually made notes. Nevertheless, there were lectures he didn't seem to know what the lecturers talked about most of the time which made the class boring and would not mind missing them so long as he had purchased their handouts to study on his own. In cases where there is no penalty for absenteeism, he would battle with learning the course himself or discussing it with his friends as that makes him understand such courses better. Lecturers who have a habit of reading out their handouts without much teaching usually puts him off.

Gradually, Ikedinachi adjusted into the university system. He attended social activities, such as departmental nights and birthdays to socialise and that allowed him to mingle more freely with girls, which worried him sometimes. He became freer with girls in class, and they found him more attractive as he was naturally endowed with unique, alluring personality.

In the hostel, he attends to his private needs and also makes out time to reflect on how he spent his day. He enjoys going through a day's experience in his head and then says his night prayer before sleeping off. He usually has a 4 a.m. alarm for early morning studies and heeds to that when favourable or he simply extends his half-sleepy arms to turn it off and continue his sleep.

His Sunday's usually begin with a mass celebration at one of the Catholic churches depending on whether he wishes to attend the early one or subsequent ones and probably the occasion at hand. Then he has the rest of the day to himself, which could be used for going out to watch football matches or movies, chatting with roommates or complete rest. He had no television, video or videotapes and found public ones interesting as it equally serves as a means of socializing.

IKedinachi lived on the campus and went home monthly or whenever he deemed it fit, which was mainly because he had to stock up on his food items and collect some money from his father.

"Mama! Mama! Brother is back," Adanna called out and ran off to welcome her brother, who came to pay them a visit from the campus. Ikedinachi hugged her and handed over to her a parcel he was carrying. They were all happy to see him home and always feel so complete whenever he is home.

He went to his father's room, and they had a brief talk before he then spent most of the night discussing with his mother and siblings. Adanna slept off while enjoying the gist and the company of her beloved ones.

"Mama, life on campus can be very challenging. Do you know that some students are not always in class for lectures and most times they pass their exams? Some students from very rich family even drive cars on campus. In fact, if you see how these students behave, you will wonder whether they are actually students or lecturers themselves. At times, I envy them."

"Eheeeh! Ikedi, don't mind them please, focus on your studies and do not allow anybody or anything to distract you. Some might come from very rich families like you said, but their parents sent them to school to study and not to show off. Like we discussed earlier, we do hear some horrible stories about campus life; how some students join bad gangs with all sorts of names and commit many atrocities all in the name of school life. No parent would wish that for their children, but it happens. It is simply because they do not heed to their parent's advice."

"Please Ikedi, do not associate with such people. Make good friends and learn from them but please be extremely careful. Always remember that you can come home anytime, we are here for you. How long will you be staying this time, till Sunday evening or Monday morning?"

"Hmmm... I would have loved to stay till Monday and leave early in the morning, but my first lecture is at 7:30 a.m. and I would like to be in class on time. So, I am going back on Sunday evening."

"Alright son, I will go and do some shopping for you first thing after breakfast. If there is anything special you want, let me know."

"Thank you, Mama. I thank God for my wonderful and loving family. I have kept you awake for so long, go and get some sleep."

"You know I can stay awake all night with you, but we both need sleep now in order to prepare for a long day ahead. Goodnight son."

"Goodnight mama."

He was happy to be home.

# Three

"**Ikedi,** how was your weekend?" Obinna asked.

"It was great. I went home on Friday evening and came back yesterday evening. How was yours?"

"Mine was not so good. I went home too but Ifeanyi my younger brother was sick, and that worried everyone. Although, this morning he felt a bit better and would be able to go to school. I came back this morning, that was why I was very late for the first lecture, but I knew that was no problem the moment I saw you in the front section."

"Oh! Poor Ifeanyi, he will be fine, don't let that disturb you much, your parents and siblings are there to give him all the support he needs. As for the lecture, we will sort that out in the evening as usual."

"It is time for the next lecture, let's hurry," Obinna ordered politely. They both left for the lecture.

Later, after classes, as they were chatting and heading towards the canteen, one of their course mates walked up to them.

"Do you mind joining me and my friend later in the evening? We will be going through that topic in the evening at 6 p.m," Obinna implored.

"That doesn't sound bad, but I would have preferred just the two of us. It's ok anyway," Ifeoma responded.

"Oh! Sorry guys, pardon my manners I did not introduce you. Ikedinachi meet Ifeoma, she is our colleague and a friend. Ifeoma meet Ikedinachi *-I prefer calling him Ikedi-* he is my close friend from secondary school, we are like brothers."

"Hi Ifeoma, nice meeting you."

"My pleasure," Ifeoma replied and they shook hands.

"Now you understand that you do not have to be worried," Obinna continued talking to Ifeoma.

Ifeoma was a bit convinced. "So, where is the venue?" she asked Obinna.

"At any nearby lit-up hall around your hostel, I think?"

He turned towards Ikedinachi, "Ikedi, what do you think?"

"Maybe she should be somewhere in front of her hostel where we can easily spot her, by then we must have figured out a better and a safer place," he added.

"Sounds better," Obinna replied.

He then said to Ifeoma, "We usually stay in our hostel but since we can't use there tonight because of you, I was kind of lost thinking of a suitable alternative. You heard my friend, so see you at 6 pm. Sorry for delaying you."

She thanked them and left for her hostel.

--

Ifeoma quickly made some food and ate it. She was just about getting some sleep when one of her roommates joined her.

"Ify, where have you been? I have checked on you several times. I wanted to join you earlier for lunch as I didn't know what to eat."

"So, you've already had something to eat?" Ifeoma struggled.

"Yes. I joined Ng; we had her left-over yam pottage."

Ifeoma continued, "I was with Obinna and his friend. You know l do ask him questions in class, I like the way he answers questions and he seems quiet in my opinion. So, I prefer going to him for clarifications."

"You know them, right?" she asked Cassandra.

"You mean the guy that was sitting beside you in class this afternoon?" Cassandra asked back.

"Yes, he was helping me out with some explanations. So, I will be meeting him and his friend this evening. He said they usually discuss different lecture topics."

"I can tell you are beginning to like this guy, are you sure it is just the lectures?" Cassandra jokingly asked.

"You are not serious Sandra. I simply like intelligent guys. He is and doesn't brag about it. It is just the lectures. Please, I must get some sleep now, it will soon be 6 pm."

'Ok, I am off, but you will explain the topics to me later or better when exams are around the corner," Sandra insisted.

"Alright, till then," Ifeoma replied. She checked the time, set an alarm and slept.

"Hi, hope your night was great," Ikedi asked Ifeoma. It was the following morning.

"Yes, it was. I liked the topics we went through last night, as well. Thanks so much. You and your friend are both brilliant."

"Thanks. We are managing," he joked.

"Do you stay around? I mean your parent's house?" "We live in Owerre, but am from Umuezeudo town."

"Oh! You are from there? We have a common boundary with your town. How come your parents chose you live that far? Well, that's University for you. You see people from different places both far and near."

"Hey! Stop sounding like we live in the Northern part of the country, Owerre is only a couple of miles away please," and they both laughed.

"I'm from Ngwo, but we live not quite far in Achafu Street."

"Achafu! I know Achafu and its noisy environment. I have heard of Ngwo so much but have not been any way near it."

"I guess you hardly come home, but now you are going to know more places since you are close to home."

Gradually the class built up, and it was lecture time. After the second lecture, they all came together.

"Obinna you were a bit late today, Ikedinachi and I had time to chat a little before the first lecture."

"Yes, but I came almost the time that lecture began."

"Hope you were ok with last night because I would like to know you didn't feel awkward during the studies?" he asked.

"It was great discussing it with intelligent guys. If I were to be by myself, those principles in Eco. and Acc. are not that easy to understand and memorise. I liked it," Ifeoma answered.

"I am glad you did," he responded.

Ikedinachi was hungry as he didn't bother to have breakfast and asked if they can join him. Ifeoma wanted to excuse herself but Ikedinachi insisted on her coming even if it's simply keeping them company. Obinna wasn't quite hungry but went with them as they normally hang out together.

Surprisingly to them, they all ate while they chatted and had a nice time. Later in the day, following a late class, they went home happily.

Ifeoma was beginning to feel attracted to these guys that she liked seeing them before and after classes as if they were the reason she attended lectures. She started worrying about what she wears to class and her makeup unlike her usual self that simply ensures she wears neat and nice clothes.

Now, she wishes to change clothes more often and look more attractive like other girls from rich families in the campus. She would like to have a different hairdo as often as she could afford to in order to look good before her friends.

She asked herself who she actually liked the most amongst these two friends but found it difficult to answer. She first knew Obinna following an incident that occurred during lecture as he mistakenly threw a pen to her in the course of passing it to a colleague that lost his. He apologised instantly and came back after classes again to let her know how sorry he really was for his careless action. That brought them to talking terms and she then started noticing him in class. He was average height, slim, fair and looked quiet. He was really nice and polite with people. He seemed to dislike hurting or making people uncomfortable or is that just how I perceive him? she soliloquized. I think I like the way he talks too.

Then, Ikedinachi came into the picture, a close friend of Obinna *-she giggled-* that he introduced me to. He is now my friend as well. Ikedinachi has a personality of his own. He is good looking, tall, dark and likes telling jokes, though not all the time. He has a good sense of humour. The other day he lured me into going to the canteen with them which turned out to be fun as I spent more time with him and I didn't regret going out with them, at all. I guess that was his charm because I can easily say no and stick to it with some other guys but that wasn't the case. I like being around him.

No, I like being around them. Both of them!

This little *drama* of hers continued in her head.

Her hostel mates kept teasing her for having a study group of boys because she tends to come back late; being that she prefers spending some time in school before retiring to the hostel and probably leave for studies in the evening as well. Initially, she was shy about it, but it was only a matter of time, she owned-up and told them to back off that she found them more intelligent and that is what matters to her.

Cassandra was her closest amongst all. She came on a fateful evening to make fun of her.

"Ify beyibe, I saw your boyfriend, he is really handsome, I see why you cannot take your eyes off him."

"Where did you see him and what was he doing?" Ifeoma asked having Ikem in mind. Ikem means my strength; her pet name for Ikedinachi which she is yet to call him.

"Hey! So, you actually have a boyfriend? I knew it because I don't trust you and those your studying antics most times."

"Sorry, I mean who did you see amongst my friends, Obinna or Ikedinachi?" Ifeoma was almost struggling and wished she hadn't replied immediately initially, but she already did.

"Ifeoma! Why are you still covering up? You think I don't know what has been going on? It is written all over you. So, can you now tell me who between the two is making you go crazy?" Cassandra teased her, but she meant every bit of it.

"Oooh!" Ifeoma responded. "Please stop calling my name like my mother. Alright, you might be right. I like them because apart from the studies, I enjoy being around them, but you have to believe me nothing that intimate is going on at the moment."

"Really? At least my guess was almost close. Besides, who did you say you will like to be very close to any time soon... am I right? Wait a minute! Who in particular do you like between the two?"

"Sandra please, I didn't say anything. I don't know," Ifeoma entreated.

"I will leave you for now but the sooner you know, the better for you."

Cassandra's parents reside in Aba, and that was where she had all her previous, basic education. She has five siblings, all boys. She is a very honest person and likes to express her feelings and views irrespective of who gets hurt and can be loud sometimes. She enjoys the company of men and likes being the centre of attraction, but it has a limit, especially when it has to do with those younger than her or ones about her age. At twenty, she already has a choice of men. She prefers older men who can lavish their money upon her and pamper her very well.

That made her wonder why her beautiful and intelligent roommate; Ifeoma, would want anything to do with mere course mates that basically have nothing to offer apart from the so-called *discussion*, she hissed.

The other day, she tried making her see reasons with her regarding her choice of men, but her colleague found the topic disturbing and probing. It worried her, but she reluctantly changed the topic.

Well, she likes Ifeoma and will not allow her preference of men come between them. She finds her very kind and generous.

As far as Cassandra is concerned, students are not for her, despite noticing that some students were living big, they couldn't just beat her choice of wealthy businessmen since they were students like her. With that always on her mind, she was off having any close relationship with any guy in the campus.

# Four

As every single day passed by, Ikedinachi felt more spellbinding to Ifeoma and longed to make it known to her. They were quite close, but he was yet to address the boyfriend-girlfriend topic properly, being that he was worried about how his friend Obinna might react to the whole issue. His friendship meant a lot to him, and he would not like to lose it. One day after lectures, he met Obinna and told him he would like them to talk about a very sensitive topic and later that day he poured his mind before his friend.

Fortunately, Obinna had always known his close friends are attracted to each other and respects their feelings. He warned his friend to be very careful and committed to the relationship as he would not like to see Ifeoma hurt or moody. They both reasoned with one another. Ikedinachi was very happy and made him understand that gaining his consent meant a lot to him as he wouldn't like to endanger their treasured friendship. They ended the chat amicably and promised to be supportive of each other at all time.

Obinna likes Ifeoma but not that he wants her for himself or perhaps, he simply opted out for his friend, being aware that he isn't ready for a one-on-one relationship at the moment. Maybe. However, he admired the fact that

Ikedinachi consulted him because few days ago, while he watched the pair when they were chatting, he felt a stench of jealousy as if his friend has snatched someone he introduced to him. If Ikedinachi had not bothered to talk about his feeling about Ifeoma with him and simply carried on as usual, he would have done nothing and probably would begin to feel uncomfortable around them, but things were different now. He was happy and dismissed that awkward feeling for good.

Obinna being a very shy guy had difficulty in asking girls out despite having lots of them as casual friends as they flocked around him owing to his gentle and caring nature. Maybe, his wooing skills were yet to be activated, so long as all men are born with it. He tends to think that he did not have what it takes to have a girl to himself. The whole idea of having a girlfriend seemed ambiguous to him. Perhaps, the girl will take over his life and begin to detect for him.

He had seen how relatives and close friends copcd with their girlfriends, the stress they go through and sometimes how they make out.

A cousin of his -Tobenna- once had him cover up for him while he was quarrelling with his '*then*' girlfriend. He played a role where he had to plead on his behalf, made up stories, and succeeded in convincing Tina. He enjoyed every bit of it. Someone observing them from a distance would think he was having the best time of his life and would easily assume that a girl he had been asking out for a very long time had accepted his request as he was all smiles and full of gestures while Tina didn't say much.

Tina continually gave him the evil look and just listened while he talked like he was doing a recitation. She knew about Obinna and had to believe him after over ten minutes of listening to his sermon. Tobenna had told him nice things about him, and that made her took his words. Not until then, she managed to smile back at Obinna; who gloated. His hard work paid off after all.

"Tell Tobe to meet me at Dee Paul's shop Saturday morning," Tina said to him.

Everyone calls Tobenna 'Tobe' for short except his parents who pronounce it in full all the time as though the meaning would depreciate if not completed.

Tobenna thanked him for having his back. He knew he could always count on Obinna. Everyone does anyway.

Obinna loved doing things his own way and was not ready for such frivolities yet. He was neither prepared to have a girl ordering his life nor willing to say no to a girl too, when that happens. Not just ready and he knew it.

--

By their third year in the University, both guys have already gotten themselves girlfriends and parade mainly in pairs around the campus most times. Despite that, their academic excellence was carried along too. Ikedinachi and Ifeoma were now an item and very fond of each other while Obinna eventually got attached to one of their junior colleagues called Cynthia. How he was able to get himself a girl that they happened not to be having lectures with, Ikedinachi could not tell.

Cynthia is short, fair in complexion, plump and intelligent; which seem to grow each day before Obinna's eyes. She spends time with Obinna mainly for academic purposes, but deep within Obinna, he knew right from the very day he met her that she was his dream girl and chose to be very close to her. Cynthia respects him so much and being the quiet type, they seem to understand each other better.

She lived in *GRA* with her parents and was the last child in her family. She has six siblings, four girls and two boys. Being the youngest, she was pampered so much. Her older siblings spoilt her with money and gifts. Despite that, she tries to behave well. One of the attributes of Enugu city is how the rich ones lived mainly in government reserved areas; commonly known as GRA. Whites previously occupied the area in the colonial days. Now, the rich have taken over, and Cynthia's parents happened to be among them. Most of the time, their driver would drop her on the campus or she would take a taxi.

In the campus, after lectures, these cliques of friends usually come together to have a chat and then schedule a time for studies and part ways. They encouraged each other and it strengthened Ikedinachi and Obinna's friendship the more.

Ifeoma and Cynthia became close friends that Cynthia regularly visited her in the hostel. Cynthia persuaded Ifeoma to visit her too.

In cynthia's house, she introduced Ifeoma as a senior departmental colleague to her family members, and told them how they made time after lectures to study. They were very impressed and pleased with her new friend and told her she can always visit.

Ifeoma could tell Cynthia was from a very wealthy home due to her dressing and needless to say, being picked up by a driver almost every day. Your parents need to be rich for a driver to come for you.

Ifeoma was pleased with the reception she got from Cynthia's family. It appeared she had told them much about her. Ifeoma comported herself properly, as usual. In her family, they are not that rich but they were raised to be contented with what they have.

As final year students, there was much academic work to do and they barely had time for flippancies. They took their studies more serious and were keen to make good grades. Nevertheless, in the hostel, Ifeoma could not help the ideas that her mind harboured. She worried about what would happen to her relationship with Ikedinachi when they leave school, whether it would continue to blossom, or they would part ways as if they never existed.

A part of her had wanted to ask Ikedinachi whether he would marry her -*jokingly*, but she found it a bit awkward to ask. Besides, in her culture, it is left for a man to ask certain questions and not the woman. This kind of question she so much wants to ask Ikedinachi is one of 'such'. She managed to suppress her thoughts and feelings and wondered if it was truly what it felt like to be in love or was something else the matter with her?

Does Ikedinachi feel this way about her? She dozed off.

Meanwhile, Ikedinachi has been fantasizing over how he would love to spend the rest of his life with Ifeoma. He was coming up with necessary plans on how they would continue to see each other after Uni, fully cognizant that Ifeoma would go back to Owerre. Then, comes their national youth service year, he sighed. He would be travelling to Owerre as often as he could, he encouraged himself.

He felt bad that he did not have enough money to lavish on his girl. He does see many couples in campus and most times wished he could bring sparks to their relationship every now and then. He managed with the little he had and fortunately for him, Ifeoma did not complain and hardly asked him for money. He counted himself lucky on that part. There are times he wondered what would happen to him if a rich man, probably a successful businessman, asked for Ifeoma's hand in marriage. It seemed impossible for him to discuss marriage with Ifeoma right now because he knew he didn't have what it takes.

This bothered ikedinachi so much that he started to articulate on how to make money fast after graduation, least he loses ifeoma to another. He will surely go mad if he should lose her. She is definitely not someone easily swayed by material things, but neither is ikedinachi going to allow such temptations. Come to think of it, "she deserves all the good things of life," he chuckled. At this, ikedinachi swore that he was going to stop at nothing to give her such a life.

# Five

**Ikedinachi** was in the canteen eating when he sighted a group of campus guys discussing what seemed to be a very important issue to them. Following long minutes of eavesdropping, he decided to join them. From what he gathered, they were discussing about ways of helping each other travel abroad, and all that revolved around it. They talked about cases whereby some students had abandoned their studies in order not to waste such a 'golden opportunity' as they termed it.

He spotted Emeka, who was the one he knew among others and he went closer to them.

"Hey! Guy, how far?" he started by greeting Emeka and then shook hands with all of them one after another. He was very careful to make sure he wasn't with the wrong set of guys and probably not at the wrong time too. Emeka excused himself from the group and left with Ikedinachi.

"What's up?" Emeka asked. "We were having an important discussion before you showed up"

"I know. I know, and I don't want to keep you for long," Ikedinachi interrupted him before he could complete his sentence.

"Em... sorry I shouldn't have listened to your discussion," Ikedinachi stammered.

"Were you guys really serious about the abroad stuff?"

Emeka could not help laughing at him. "Of course, we are. I can't believe anyone can ask such a dumb question. Do we look like small boys to you?" Emeka bluffed.

"I will have to go back now, we shall discuss later during the week."

"Alright. Thanks," Ikedinachi said and left for the hostel.

"Sorry guys I'm back," Emeka pleaded with his colleagues. "Hope I did not miss any vital information?" He sat down and joined the discussion once more.

They were almost through and were about to go their separate ways before one of them asked.

"Mekus, who was that guy and what does he want?"

"He is a friend. He somehow overheard us and seems interested."

"Hahaha!" they all laughed.

"He thinks we deal with poor boys, tell him it involves raw Cash. Money!"

They went their separate ways.

As Ikedinachi headed towards the hostel, he thought of the guys he just met and how they knew much about abroad despite being students like him. He shook his head and said to himself that if it was a genuine idea that he would like to be part of it. He has always dreamed big about life. Moreover, if there is a place better than his country, he would love to know what that place looks like if luck is on his side.

It was as though he had forgotten every other thing going on around him as his thoughts were now filled with what life would be abroad. The next day, he saw Obinna and broke the news to him, but to his greatest surprise, Obinna was not excited about the whole idea. Ikedinachi had wanted to plan with him and hoped their plans work out but not when Obinna seemed apathetic. He tried to seek his opinion. Obinna has no relative abroad, and the idea of living outside his country sounded strange to him. He preferred a calm and calculated lifestyle, unlike Ikedinachi who is adventurous.

"I don't think I'm interested, I can't handle such thoughts now. Besides, where do I start from?" "Well, if everything works out for you, I wouldn't mind paying you a visit." "You and Ifeoma, right?" he asked Ikedinachi.

Ikedinachi was not happy with the kind of response he got from his friend. He made him understand that he had told him because he thought it was a wonderful idea and he didn't want to keep it from him but since he was not interested and did not support him, he would try and see what he could make out of it all.

Obinna felt bad and apologized to him. He told him not to misunderstand him and assured him that he has his full support. He equally warned him to ascertain that Emeka and his colleagues were being honest before getting involved with them.

Ikedinachi agreed with him and made him understand that he had that in mind as he still has a long time to decide what he wanted and then make a decision.

"When was the last time you went home Ikedi? I might be going this weekend."

"I intend to, but in case I change my mind, you would help me deliver a message to my mother and get something from her in return."

"Alright. Will let you know before I leave the Campus." Their friendship had flourished that it has resulted in their families relating well at home. They have become family friends.

"Have you seen Cynthia today?"

"Maybe, she doesn't have lectures today," Ikedinachi replied.

"She told me she would be in school. I will hang around and wait for her."

Obinna love Cynthia to bits. He laughs when he hears people talk about love at first sight and thinks you really need to know someone, their personality and character before the emergence of walking into the path of love. The whole boy-and-girl-love topic is a big deal for him. However, from the first time he saw Cynthia, he felt attracted to her in a way that he couldn't quite describe, which was very strange to him. He allowed the strange attraction to overpower him.

He had watched her from afar for a while and decided to talk to her. He walked close to her and was almost walking at the same pace as her before he was able to utter a word. He introduced himself and asked her if she needed some company. Her answer would not matter as he was willing to walk her all day so long as she was going to talk to him. Cynthia did not mind the company she had, and they both headed to the stationary shop she was going to.

Obinna was amazed by the aura that surrounds her too. Her gazes were like charm; and when they came, he felt blown away, he had not spotted that from afar. He helped her to carry her book folder; it looked heavy the way she had carried it.

"Do you bring this much books to school every day? You must be a serious student," Obinna asked. Anything to make a conversation with her was considered.

"Yes, I do. At times, the ones I leave behind would be the ones I would really want to use." Her voice was so angelic, she talked in a very soft tone and dragged her words like each one was very important. She sounded like she was singing; she has a soothing voice that can make an angry man freeze and make a baby fall asleep. Maybe that is the way the rich people sound due to too much TV.

She was worth all the efforts. From that day, he began to check on her and Cynthia liked his company as he was ahead of her and was intelligent too.

Over time, he got so used to having her around, they became inseparable. He enjoyed walking her to where she gets a taxi or keeping her company till the driver comes to pick her. He longs for their chats after lectures as though it was a ritual that needed to be observed perpetually. They would either sit side by side or walk hand in hand, whatever the case may be, those moments Obinna tends to be in the best planet - *Jupiter*.

---

In the hostel, most of the girls just came back from weekend, and as usual, had lots of spicy gists.

Cassandra was the happiest amongst all. She was talking and singing out loud almost the same time while unpacking her belongings. She made sure she displayed all her new clothes by hanging them on a wooden wall hanger nailed to the wall.

"Ifeoma can you spare me some minutes? I have some hot news for you," she shouted from her corner of the room.

"Really? I'm here," Ifeoma replied. Ifeoma had finished sweeping and was unpacking her suitcase. She was very happy with the number of foodstuffs her mother bought for her and was placing them in different containers to ensure she did not run out at the same time.

"Ify, my weekend was so, so sweet. You needed to see me," Cassandra said to Ifeoma as she slumped to the bed and made herself comfortable.

"Hey! You came back with all these food items? That means you were carrying a very heavy load."

"We will not go hungry anytime soon; our final days are going to be the best."

"Didn't you come back with loads?" Ifeoma asked although she is used to her friend's sarcastic way of talking.

"I did, but it was more of clothes. You know I prefer collecting money for food items than buying them at home and bringing it back to school."

"Ok. So, can I hear the hot gist?" Ifeoma asked while they both enjoyed some banana and groundnut she bought on her way back to school.

"Do you remember that my tall Lagos boyfriend? Not the one that lives in Aba that visited last month," Cassandra asked her.

"Yes. Yes, I remember him now, the one that bought that expensive wristwatch for you."

"Hmmm... he asked for my hand in marriage and I accepted. He met my parents during the weekend," she continued looking very excited.

"I am so happy he is very rich, at least amongst all other men I know."

"This calls for celebration, congratulations!" Ifeoma was very happy for her friend.

"I am delighted that you have found love at last."

"What? Did I mention love to you? Ify, he has money and cares about me. I know once we are married, we are going to live happily, that's how I see life and *love*."

"I know you know a lot more about love than me, but I'm not bothered. Keep loving," she added in a sarcastic manner.

"We will be getting married after my graduation, and you must be there."

"Why not? I would not miss it for anything," Ifeoma smiled. "I will make it despite the distance. Till then, we are going to have much time to plan."

"Come, let me show you most of the things he bought for me. You can choose the ones you like, apart from the handbag." Cassandra stood up and lead the way.

Ifeoma joined her as she went to her corner in the room.

"All these beautiful clothes for you, you better start selling some," Ifeoma teased her. "I can see your fiancé is very caring indeed."

"I told you, he is," Cassandra replied. She hung down some clothes to show Ifeoma how beautiful they looked and tried her favourites.

"They are lovely, aren't they?" she asked.

"They are. You look stunning in them, I'm chuffed. He does know what fits you so well."

By now, Cassandra had succeeded in scattering her clothes everywhere; on the bed, table, and the floor. They were both exhausted and retired to their beds after bouts of gossips.

---

Weeks had gone by, and Ikedinachi was yet to see Emeka, and that made him much more worried coupled with the fact that they would soon be leaving school.

"How far, Obi," he greeted Obinna after classes as he headed towards him.

"I'm alright. What's up?"

"Good. I have not seen that Emeka since then."

"Really? Don't allow that to disturb you; he might come around one of these days. Hey, I want to check on Cynthia before she leaves campus. See you later."

"Oh! My regards to her," he said as Obinna left.

Ifeoma hurriedly walked into the class. She had left earlier with Cassandra and friends to buy some snacks and signaled Ikedinachi that she would return.

"Sorry Ikem, hope I did not keep you waiting for so long?"

"No."

"Cassandra my friend is getting married soon and is happy as a clam. I couldn't have possibly refused going out with them."

"No problem, Obinna stayed with me briefly, he left almost seconds before you came in. Cassandra? That's good news. I mean good for her. We will get married sometime," he laughed.

"Yes, her husband to be is a rich businessman in Lagos and spoils her with money and gifts." Ifeoma was willing to discuss her friend further with Ikedinachi before he switched to a different subject.

"That's good. Ify, hope you are not hungry, do you want to have something?" he asked fully aware that she just had something but felt he needed to act like the nice guy.

"I've had gala and fanta. I'm filled up. I brought gala for you too," she offered it to him.

"You bought for me? Thanks." He took it from her.

Ikedinachi told Ifeoma about how he ran into Emeka and his clique couple of weeks ago and was hoping for better and more clarification in subsequent meetings with Emeka.

"I was going to tell you earlier after getting more information from him. What do you think?" he asked, looking at her to see her reaction to the odd topic.

"Hmmm... it's ok," she said in no particular tone.

"You are full of surprises," her eyes widened. "And you are worried that you have not seen him, do not tell me that you are willing to abandon studies for abroad?"

"Not really, but I need to know what is involved so that I can plan towards it."

"Ikem, going abroad is a good idea, but I would like you to graduate first and do not forget we still have a year after studies for national youth service. You cannot abandon all of these. Can you?"

"No, not that I can say for now."

Luckily for him, he saw Emeka the next day, but all did not seem well.

"Hi, I have searched everywhere for you. You have not been coming to school, are you alright?"

Emeka had issues with some guys in the campus, and things have not been so smooth for him. He knew why Ikedinachi has been eager to see him.

"I'm ok. How much do you have? I would like to know before we delve into the topic."

"Am a student like you. I don't think I have that kind of money you want to hear. Please tell me all that I need to know so that I can start working towards it."

"I should have known," Emeka hissed.

"It requires much money, when you are ready, you know where to find me."

"Is that all you are going to tell me?" he asked him while scratching his head at the same time. He felt disappointed.

"And where do I find you?"

"When you go to that short, fat Calabar woman's restaurant, where you saw us the other time, ask after one of her girls, Ekaette, she will tell you my whereabouts, that is if am still in the Country by then o." *He stretched the last part.*

"She will provide you with the latest information."

"I'm off. See you when you are ready," he dashed off.

# Six

**Upon** the completion of their studies, they all parted ways. Cynthia was now in her final year and the only one left behind in college. She has made a couple of friends in school and surprisingly to her, she seemed to be enjoying school life the more.

Prior to Obinna's graduation, she had thought campus life would be boring without her Obinna. In his last days, she became ill. It was as if her body systems were shutting down. She became depressed, would not eat properly, and was withdrawn. Surprisingly, two months later things turned around.

It was as though she recovered and suddenly found herself in a new university. People that do not usually talk to her for one reason or the other had developed special eyes for her and even threw jokes at her. She enjoyed every bit of the attention she got. As a last child in her family with grown-up siblings, she enjoys attention a lot, likes being pampered, and dislikes isolation and harsh voices. Her smallish stature meant she was liked by many as she was quiet and did not in any way appear intimidating.

On one occasion after a lecture, while chatting with groups of friends, she jokingly asked them why they never talked to her back then.

"Ha! I do not want any form of trouble; I don't usually trust quiet guys, they can be mean most times," Charles replied.

"You don't usually stay behind with us and" one of her colleagues added before being interrupted by Cynthia.

"So, my boyfriend was the reason? Good to know. Well, I would like to think I played a part too."

"I am still with him!" she shouted. "But I enjoy your company too please," she begged them.

Charles was the one she liked the most among them. She found most of the qualities she admired in Obinna in him. Of advantage to him, he loved cracking jokes, very loving and could neither be classified as a quiet nor strident guy. When they were together, they hardly experienced a dull moment and always made each other happy. They enjoyed each other's company even when they did not discuss any particular topic of interest.

Just like Obinna, Charles would walk her to the junction where she gets a taxi. She was not the type of girl that takes a guy to her house, and that was not a norm in their place too. Not even Obinna had visited her in her parents' house. The act of walking her had become a routine to the extent that Cynthia had already become fond of him unbeknown to her.

This time, it was different, if she was not laughing on the top of her voices, she would be tickled. She enjoyed times spent with Charles. She loves all the attention she gets.

Obinna endeavoured to see her whenever he was around as he travelled often to deliver supplies for his father, who is a distributor to two companies based in Enugu. At least, that earned him some money for basic necessities until he went for youth service. They hung out in restaurants, and Obinna was not bothered and knew that he would get to know her house and meet her parents at the appropriate time.

Their favourite restaurant was a nearby Mr Biggs, where some of the old waiters already knew them as a pair owing to the fact that they appeared to be regular and sat at a particular spot, except in the very few instances it was occupied by other customers.

On one of their meetings, Obinna felt very attracted to Cynthia in a way that he had never thought of possible. He told Cynthia that he would wait for her to complete her studies and would then marry her. He told her that it would give him time to make some money and be prepared for marriage and all that it entails.

Cynthia couldn't help how she felt while she listened to her boyfriend saying what glowed her heart. She giggled and told him that she loves him so much, and that would be a dream come true for her.

As they chatted further, Obinna explained to her how he had been managing and how difficult life could be after school.

"I have applied for jobs in different places and have been called for a few interviews. But after a long time, guess what?"

"I am listening, why don't you go ahead and tell me. You know I can be horrible at making guesses. Please..." she pleaded.

They both laughed.

"Ok, let me make an attempt. You were successful in one of the interviews and have been asked to go and work in Lagos?" she asked spreading out her palms in a childish manner.

Obinna began laughing loudly now and was not bothered whether other people were staring or not.

"You were very close. Fair attempt!" he shouted.

"I was successful. I am going to work with a firm in Enugu here and will be resuming work next month."

Cynthia screamed and hugged him tightly and affectionately while Obinna held her back and never wanted to let go.

They had a lovely time and did not like saying goodbye, but it must be said at some point. It was almost 7 pm and already dark.

"Lest I forget, hope you still hear from your friends Ikedi and Ifeoma?"

"Yes. It's been a while since I last saw him though."

"I guess they should be doing fine."

"Ok," she added.

Obinna saw her off, and they fixed a time and date for their next meeting. He hurriedly got to the motor park because he needed to get a taxi before their closing time. He didn't like keeping late nights but not on a day like that when he felt the hours of the day needed to be lengthened.

It was very dark when he got home as it was about one-hour journey. He was very tired as well and had to calm his worried parents down. He had his dinner and went straight to bed.

At home, Cynthia was unnecessarily excited that one could tell something was responsible for her ecstatic mood.

She carried out tasks happily without grumbling or seeking for help from her elder ones.

While she was with Obinna, she was comparing Obinna to Charles, but her Obinna remained at the top.

"How cunny the heart can be," she said to herself.

A part of her felt like she was cheating on Obinna. Obinna was her boyfriend, and Charles was good friend and a course mate -*the right adjective was not fast coming.*

"Yes, he is a *good-friend-course-mate.* We are just friends that care about each other, and nothing more is attached to that."

"Moreover, he has not spelt anything out to me, and I have done nothing wrong that am supposed to feel guilty about," Cynthia fought with her conscience.

"Cynthia!" her elder sister called out.

"Yes!" she ran off.

# Seven

**Ikedinach**i and Ifeoma had survived the storm of national service year, which took place in the Kaduna and Lagos respectively. Fortunately for Ifeoma, she was retained in the bank where she served while Ikedinachi left Kaduna and would not have stayed back even if they had retained him because he did not like the northern part of the country. Cassandra on the other hand was now living in Lagos with her husband and worked in the same bank with her friend.

The day Cassandra resumed work was a great day for them as they never thought fate would bring them back together after all those years back at university. They were a shoulder to lean on for one another despite their personality clashes. They realised how supportive of each other they were at the University and missed the old lovely times, which separation following their graduation brought about. Ifeoma had longed to see her and to ask how she was faring as a married woman. She had always thought to herself that for some strange reasons, when people get married, their attitude and values become transformed automatically.

The last time they had seen each other was on Cassandra's wedding day which Ifeoma was able to honour against all odds. Initially, her parents were of the opinion that since she was not the maid of honour, why must she be there as they found travelling to Lagos very far; that alone worried and disturbed them. She told them that Cassandra had been her best friend and she would be part of her 'Ashebi' with other colleagues residing in Lagos. She tried earnestly to convince them, and they reluctantly gave in, wishing she could change her mind.

Cassandra's wedding was one in town. The entire celebration took place at Holy Trinity Catholic Church in Festac town. The reception saw many faces especially those of influential men and women with their corresponding big bellies and massive arses, who flaunted money like they did not encounter any form of hard work while generating it. They all looked glamorous and indeed made the wedding a very colourful one. Ifeoma found every aspect of the wedding captivating, right from the exchange of vows in the church to the 'dance, dance, dance' during reception. She had little time to chat with Cassandra and was able to meet Onyema, her husband, 'the rich Lagos businessman' she had heard so much about. He was not as old as she expected, although she knew Cassandra can be horrible in exaggerating issues. She found them both lovely as a couple and was sure that he was exactly the kind of man that could tame her friend. He was pleased to meet her, and he told her that his wife had told him much about her-*in a concentrated igbo accent*. They exchanged pleasantries before she left to catch a night bus back to Owerre.

"Ify! Who am I seeing?" asked Cassandra when she saw Ifeoma behind the desk.

"Is this real?"

"Sandra! long time. Please tell me you work here."

Ifeoma stood from her desk and walked towards her. They hugged each other and could not stop bickering. In such instances, Cassandra does not give a damn who she disturbs. Ifeoma was signaling her to lower her voice. There was a meeting of financial executives going on in the other section of the building and Ifeoma would not like them to be heard.

"This is my first day. I hope it does not look stressful as it sounds?"

"No, I don't think so. Nice having you here. I have always remembered the old wonderful memories. I served here and was retained afterwards."

"Oh! I should have remembered because you mentioned it back then. Lucky you! Does that mean this bank is really good or just the big-name factor?"

"In my opinion, it is good. I don't know how others see it but I'm sure you are going to like it."

"How is your husband? You look great, married woman," Ifeoma added. They both laughed. Obviously, they seem to have lots of catching up to do.

"He is good. He does not want me to work. Can you imagine that?"

"Really? He doesn't want you to suffer, I guess. The thing is, one really needs to practice, else what is the essence of going to the University?"

"So, you know! Initially, I agreed. You know how I was in school, always thinking less about many ideas, but I had an encounter during my service year. I ran into some women whose marriage and life has taken different dimensions because they were all dependent on their husbands. It truly changed my views. Moreover, I cannot cope with staying at home even when the money overflows, I'm still young and do not want to retire at this early stage. Huh!"

"It was a serious argument Ify. I said to him, why would you marry me and expect me not to work after all my education?"

"I am not surprised because most rich men do not allow their wives to work. It is nice you were able to convince him."

"Eheee! Are you still with that your school-boyfriend?" Cassandra asked in a tone that actually meant '*I do not know what you are still doing with that poor guy and I can't tell when you are going to get married.*'

"Yes, we are fine." Ifeoma smiled and shook her head. "Cassandra, you have not changed one bit."

They went back to their offices and carried on with their work before closing time drew close.

Within two months, Ikedinachi succeeded in getting a job with a firm in Lagos, and that meant he would have no problem of distance in his relationship with Ifeoma, at least for the time being. They were both pleased to have each other around and in a more suitable way as working class than school lovers. They utilised their leisure time very well. People seeing them for the first time could mistake them for new lovers as their love seemed to be stronger every single day. It was as though the separation during their service year had ignited their passion.

They made sure they made time to meet most weekends. Ifeoma was very grateful for the man she had fallen in love with. To her, Ikedinachi's behaviour had almost become predictable just as night follows day. They grew very fond of each other and continually shared dreams of their-would-be-future together.

However, working life was very different from school life. They exchanged visits as often as they could. Ikedinachi most times do mistake himself for a married man being that he felt at home with the world in his current situation. Whereas, on some occasions, Ifeoma would feel like she had overstepped her boundaries as a young Christian girl that enjoyed holding her morals high.

As far as she is concerned, there are certain levels of fun that should be reserved till marriage but not to Ikedinachi who likes trying all tricks in the book, except the ones he doesn't know.

One evening, Ikedinachi was worried and tried to mask his feeling before Ifeoma, but she did not give in to it.

"Ikem, what is bothering you?" "Did you get any message from home?" Ifeoma asked in a very soft tone.

"No, I didn't. It's just…" he paused. "You remember I mentioned back then to you at Uni about those guys that organise trips abroad?" "Do you remember the story?"

"Yes, what about them?" "They didn't seem to be honest, and you felt disappointed and em…."

"I have always thought about the trip. Now, there is this guy in my workplace that is connected to some abroad agents." He sat upright.

"He told me that it is genuine and that some people including those he knows have travelled through them. He also mentioned one of our colleague that is processing his and wants me to join them as I indicated interest. I even told him my previous story. He has already made few contacts for me and said my travelling documents would be ready within the next three months."

Ifeoma looked flushed. She was confused and couldn't explain how she felt. It was a mixed feeling; it was good that he would be going abroad like he always wanted but not like this, not so sudden.

*"What would happen to their relationship?"* Her head was almost exploding.

Ikedinachi folded his arms around her and held her tightly. She tried to pull away but couldn't.

"Ify, I understand how you feel and that is exactly my problem. I have always wanted this trip, and now it seems to be happening, but it all seems clouded."

"Please look at me straight in the eyes," he raised her chin. "I love you and nothing will ever change that. I need you, we are going to plan this and our future together. I don't care what it involves."

"If marrying you now would make things much easier for us, I don't mind."

Ifeoma pulled out from him, wanting to know if he was actually in his right senses.

"Ikem, are you serious with what you have just said? How long have you been keeping these ideas from me? Please, just give me some time to think about what my ears just heard. I don't think I can handle further news." She was now sobbing and insisted on going back to her place.

"I am so sorry, I did not mean it to be this way, please reason with me. I am not feeling any better," Ikedinachi Pleaded.

"I have not been keeping anything away from you. It all happened during the week, and considering the time frame, I have to think very fast. I need your opinion please...

Ifym." Ikedinachi was trying to fight back his emotions as tears filled his own eyes too.

"I will give you some time, if that is what you want. We are going to discuss better next time and see what happens from there. Besides, I am yet to travel to tell my parents."

"Ify please we need to be strong now. I love you."

Ifeoma was speechless and only nodded her head.

Ikedinachi boarded a taxi with her to make sure she got home safely. They strangely had no conversation while in the cab. He made sure she was ok and then left for his house. Their weekend would have been fun as usual if not for the topic he chosen to discuss, but he didn't regret it because it was a crucial one.

It was as though the night was twenty hours on its own. Ifeoma was apparently awake all through the night. She couldn't differentiate between dreams and fantasies. She so much wanted to fall deeply asleep, but sleep was far from her.

She was so grumpy at work that her colleagues noticed that something was troubling her. Despite that, she was able to carry out her official duties. She tried as much as she could not to tell any of them what troubled her. She did not like sharing her problems with people except with very close friends and family.

"Ify Baby, what is the problem? I have noticed that all is not well since Monday." Muyiwa asked.

"Nothing you should worry about, thanks for your concern. I'm glad you asked."

"Anyway, I am much better now," she put up a smiling face and tried to be brave.

"If you say so, I will let you be."

Muyiwa figured out that she obviously did not want to tell him whatever the problem was. He had liked her right from the first time they carried out a task together in the office. He found her charming and well reserved; his typical definition of a woman. He is a bachelor and yet to be committed in any relationship. He kept telling himself he had not seen the kind of girl that would sweep him off his feet.

He has tried a couple of times to gain Ifeoma's attention and did sound nice, though not in a flirtatious way; which he would have loved.

He began to check her out.

# Eight

**Ikedinachi** celebrated over numerous recent events and agonised that there were more that needed to get done in limited time. He needed to have a word with his girlfriend and make a trip to Enugu to discuss the situation of things with his parents as it was not the kind of subject he could easily write and send to them. He was convinced that marrying Ifeoma would be the best decision he had made so far in his life. He thought of how things could change while he would be away and how he would always keep in touch until she joins him, *if only wishes were horses, beggars would ride.* He sighed in relief.

Travelling abroad had always been his dream ever since his university days because he came from an average family and would like to change the condition of things in his family. On the other hand, setting up a viable business which was his initial plan requires a lot of capital which he has sadly realised. The appalling situation of Nigerian Naira didn't help matters either as it has turned blue collar jobs into dreaded ditches where employees end up borrowing into their next pay check before it arrives, even for a university graduate like himself, he chuckled. He couldn't imagine his family struggling through this financial quagmire.

It won't be easy to make it oversees either but stands a much better chance especially for a hardworking fellow like himself. "After all, that's why Papa and Mama called me "Ikedinachi", he told himself. There was no way he was going to miss this golden opportunity. He was lost in thought but very optimistic all through.

He had a mental map of what he was going to do and how he would get them done. He can drag his feet at times but usually performs his best when trying to beat a deadline. And this was the case. He had made up his mind on how he would convince his parents and get them to reason with him and possibly encourage him.

He went over to Ifeoma's place for a proper chat. This time around they discussed deeply what mattered to them. Ifeoma had some time to think straight too.

"Why London? Who goes there? The people I knew that travelled to London barely came home. Besides, it takes them forever to build a house – *that is, if they ever do.* What happened to the United States of America, Canada, and other beautiful places of the world? People from England only blow grammar. *No kobo,*" Ifeoma fumed as she went on.

In her heart, she wanted to scream 'What about us? What happens to me? Don't you know I can't cope without you?' But she did not voice these particular opinions of hers – *if only Ikedinachi had become a wizard to read minds.* She remembered one of her other's popular sayings 'a woman is meant to be reserved.' All the time? She would normally reply. One thing was for sure, she did not like the whole travelling overseas idea at all.

Ikedinachi almost felt like laughing but not on such topics, especially as he wanted to sound very serious and convince her. He truly needs her validation. He loved and cherished her.

Ikedinachi told her he would like them to get married as soon as possible and hoped she would join him when he would have sorted himself out while overseas.

"Ifym, I have always admired England as a nation, their way of living and all the stories about the royal family. The country is known for quality education. I know I will have to work hard to make money. I will give it my best. I have some respect for people from that country and really would love to be there." He paused for few seconds and continued.

"We are going to be fine okay?"

Reluctantly but happily, Ifeoma reasoned with him as she could not think of her life without him and couldn't bear allowing him to travel without any commitment. It was as though the timing seemed right for them. She accepted his marriage proposal and they were over the moon.

Ikedinachi further told her that he would be travelling to the east to explain the whole situation to his parents and then meet his future in-laws for the first time, which meant Ifeoma would need to travel too. They were excited and spent the whole weekend together before he left for Enugu on Monday. He had previously taken permission from work.

During lunch at work, Ifeoma told Cassandra the whole story; which she found wonderful and weird at the same time. It was wonderful because her friend would soon marry and probably become an abroad lady soonest, and weird being that they were all too sudden, she could not tell how long Ikedi was going to abandon her friend in the country. Why was it that she couldn't find herself a well-to-do man, she thought?

However, she encouraged her and told her to make her aware of their wedding date as soon as she could as she would love to be there. Ifeoma promised to do so, despite knowing that there could be delays in delivery of letters sometimes. They had a girly gossip and Ifeoma felt a lot better and thanked her for being a true friend.

"Ify, send the wedding card through the Onyeije Motors in Apama Park. Print Onyema Ndu on it. My husband usually sends goods through them and they arrive weekly."

"Thanks! Thanks." Ifeoma put in. "I have actually thought of how fast to reach you." She noted the name carefully.

Ifeoma was able to obtain a leave of absence from work and travelled the next weekend. Not that her managers refusal would have stopped her from travelling anyway.

Monday had passed and Muyiwa was yet to set his eyes on Ifeoma. He wondered whether she was sick and needed some help or something else. On Wednesday, he went to Cassandra to find out her friend's whereabouts.

"Sandra, how is your day going?"

"Fine and yours?" in a tone that meant this one you walked up to my desk to ask how I am.

"Good. I like your shirt."

"Thanks!"

"Eh... sorry. *This one* Ifeoma has not been coming to work, is she alright?"

"Yes, she is. She took permission."

"Oh! It was planned. I was thinking it was a sort of emergency."

"Do you know her reason? Sorry when is she coming back to work?"

"She travelled to east and would come back when she needs to be back," she said in a no-joke tone and knew she was sounding harsh.

"Sorry, why do you care when she comes back?"

Muyiwa intended to find out more from her but certainly not from the way she responded to him.

"Is it wrong to ask after a colleague you have not seen lately at work? Thanks for the information though," and he left her.

Cassandra felt she shouldn't have talked to him like that, but the deed was done. She knew he admired Ifeoma.

Muyiwa is a dark, not so slim, tall guy with charming dentition. He talked in a calm manner like a *player*.

Cassandra was not happy that he wasn't the one that had met her friend all these while and now she has gone to cement a relationship with Ikedinachi, he came to ask her after her.

"Mtchew!" Perhaps, she simply admired him and cannot have him since she is married. And that was one of her tools in dealing with such instances.

The week went by, whenever she ran into Muyiwa they simply exchanged greetings, and she kept restraining herself from apologising about her attitude the previous week.

# Nine

**Ikedinachi's** parents and siblings were delighted with having Ikedinachi home after a long time. He gave them the gift items which he had brought from Lagos.

"Ikedi my son, you look very big now. Is it just the Lagos? Or work? Well, whichever one it is, it surely treats you well."

"You bought all these for us, clothes, handbag, shirts..." Mrs. Okoro asked him as she sang, danced and showered him with praises while she unfolded the *abada* he bought for her.

"May God continue to bless and keep you for us." She was very pleased with the mere sight of seeing her son. She kept running her eyes over him; assessing and admiring him from head to toe.

Adanna was overly excited with the pink canopy dress and red handbag he bought for her. She wore them immediately and was showed off her latest additions. She played with her handbag and was very happy that it had a mirror in it too. Ikedinachi was happy to know she liked them being that he did not know her choice and wasn't with Ifeoma at the time he pick them, who could have helped him

59

out. Meanwhile, he bought a few shirts for Ugonna, which he liked. They all saw him as a blessing to the family.

Ikedinachi had greeted his father earlier when he arrived and now joined him in the palour. Mr. Okoro was watching the NTA 9 pm news on the television. He gently dropped a bottle of Schnapp hot drink and a case containing a wristwatch he bought for him on the table in front of him. The expensive wrist-watch almost took all his first salary, but he knew it was worth it.

"Papa this is what I brought from Lagos," he handed out the drink to him with both hands.

His father collected it.

"And this," Ikedinachi added. He gave him the wrist-watch.

Mr. Okoro's hands were filled with gifts from his son.

He opened the watch case and was proud of his son's choice.

"Thank you, my son. You have done so well."

"Papa, I hope you like it? I bought it with my first salary."

"I love it, my son. I never dreamt of wearing such an expensive wristwatch."

"You bought *this-rich-men* watch for your poor Father? May you never lack! May the almighty God continue to guide and bless you. You will get a good wife. You will have kids as many as you wish and they will care for you too."

He kept showering blessings upon his son.

"Hope you have only come to see us or is there any issue you want to discuss with your father? You are home on a Monday, hope all is well?" His father interjected, "Are you on leave?"

"Eheeee... no papa, I, I actually took permission from work," he was battling with words and almost wanted to claim that he was on leave but thought it needless.

"I will talk about it tomorrow papa, I have a couple of days to stay. Let me not keep you awake; I wouldn't like to deprive you of your sleep." He still battled with his words.

"Well, if you say so, tomorrow then. May the day break, my son." His father was nearly drawn aback by his response but wanted to allow him talk to him when he wished. Like he already told him, he had a couple of days to stay and therefore needed not to be rushed. He stood up and joined his wife in their bedroom.

"May the day break, papa." Ikedinachi felt a relief as he almost choked knowing that his father almost caught him off guard.

He went to bed. His mother would have loved to chat with him that night as usual, but she decided to allow him rest after such a long journey from Lagos.

In the room, Adanna was deep asleep while Ugonna had been waiting for him.

"Brother, how is Lagos? I have heard so much about there and would like to live there." He has completed his secondary education and was due to go to University.

"Lagos is a very big and beautiful place. It is a rich man's land," he teased his kid brother. "That reminds me, have you taken any exams yet?"

"Yes, I took one. Still waiting for the result."

"Good, Ugoo let's talk tomorrow I need to get some sleep now."

"Alright brother, sleep well."

Ikedinachi turned over, facing the wall, he fell asleep.

The next day, Mrs. Okoro had arrived from the market and later joined Ikedinachi in the palour.

"Ikem how is Lagos?"

"Lagos is fine mama. Mama I want us to discuss a very important issue, and that is why I came back."

"Hey! Hope there is no problem my son!" she screamed placing her two hands on her chest.

"Are you having problem with anybody?"

"No mama, it is nothing near that. I will be travelling overseas very soon, and would like to...."

Mrs. Okoro could not believe what she was hearing. She left her own sofa and came and sat next to him. She could not shout anymore.

*"Huh! Obodo oyibo kwa?"* She supported her jaw with her left hand while looking at her son with utmost surprise. It was obvious he had many things lined up to say, and she listened anxiously.

"There is a girl I have known while I was at University, I would like to marry her before I travel."

On hearing this, Mrs. Okoro went back to her previous seat.

"Are you through with your listings? Ikedinachi!" she stood up this time.

"Yes, mama," he replied in a quiet tone knowing the situation he has placed her mother in.

"Hey!!!" she screamed and bit her finger, "Ikedinachi you will not kill me with hypertension in this house? Have you told your father about this?" she walked from one end of the room to another.

"No mama. That's is why I'm telling you first so that you can help me convince Papa." He looked into his mother's eyes as if his mother's eyes emit some rays that transform one's reasoning.

"Ikedi nwam! If it were to be in the olden days when majority of the people were Pagans, I would have sent you for proper cleansing by the gods long, long ago." She snapped her right fingers three times.

"Oh! You knew you needed to be supported?" Mrs. Okoro was restless, "and you did not know exactly where to start?".

At first, she was somewhat delighted to hear about travelling abroad, knowing it meant well not only for him but the entire family. The thought of her son getting married was overwhelming for her as she couldn't wait to carry her own grandchild, but she had plans for him. That notwithstanding, *but why all at the same time*? she wondered. Her son presented the issues in a very uncomfortable way. The whole idea appeared messy in her head.

"Why can't you deal with issues like these one at a time in that head of yours, eh?" She was shouting.

"Please mama, I truly need your support this present time. It is hard for me too, but I need to do what I need to do. I love Ifeoma, and I know you will love her too when you meet her. She is very nice and comes from a good Catholic family too. I do not want to lose her for any reason, and that is the main reason why I have decided to marry her now."

*"Bia nwoke m, O di ime?"* - is she pregnant? Inquired Mrs. Okoro in her native dialect, still not convinced on the reason for the rush.

"No Mama"

"Hum! Ehee! Did you say she is a very nice girl? How do you know a nice woman, Ikedi? I have been telling mama

Ndidiamaka, my neighbour in the market that we will come and meet his family this Christmas, and you were busy finding yourself a wife."

"Mama, mama, please do not go there," Ikedinachi did not give her the chance to go further. He sat up.

"You should have known right from time that nobody can decide for me on whom to marry. I have taken your words so many times but not this time," he let out in a very bitter tone thinking it might be best if he simply waits and discuss with his father later.

"Mama, let's discuss later, I will talk to papa when he comes back." He was making his way outside to get some fresh air before his mother stopped him. She suddenly realised she had overreacted.

"Ikem, so where is this Ifeoma from?"

"Umuezeudo," he sighed and sat down again.

"Umuezeudo?" She seemed unhappy on hearing the name of the town but tried not to raise her voice anymore. She has heard some ill stories about most of Umuezeudo women and cannot be deceived by its name.

"Where does her parents live?"

"Owerre."

"You mean she grew up in Owerre?" she asked in relief because most inhabitants of Owerre tend to be responsible and value education.

"Yes, mama."

"Who knows what this *could-be-wayward* Umuezeudo girl must have done to my son?" she thought. After a marathon of questions and answers all in a bid to know Ifeoma and her family well, they both dispersed as time for Mr. Okoro's arrival from work drew near and dinner was yet to be prepared. She was carried away by the long unending and not-ended chat with her son.

Later in the night, Ikedinachi walked into the sitting room and joined his father who has been listening to the news.

"Papa, how was work today?" he asked to gain his attention while he made himself comfortable in the sofa having tactfully planned on how to get his father to agree with him without much hassle.

"It went well my son." They sat for few minutes without saying a word to each other before he broke the silence.

"What is it you said you are going to tell me?"

"Yes, papa. I thought you needed some time..." he scratched the left side of his head and began.

"Emm.... Papa, I would like to travel to overseas soon and I have made all the necessary arrangements for that." He looked at his father to know his reaction but got nothing. That gave him a little confidence.

"And... I would like to marry a girl I have known for some time now, before I travel."

Mr. Okoro smiled but said nothing. Ikedinachi was relieved that he had been able to pass the message across within a minute despite not getting a response yet.

"Hmmm... are you through son?" his father asked in very calm manner. He took a deep breath.

"Yes, papa," he said rubbing his palms of his hands together.

"That's good son. You are doing well for yourself. Where in overseas?"

"London in England."

"And how soon is it?"

"In the next three months, I shall be ready. A colleague at work connected me and has made serious preparation in regards to leaving almost the same time when my traveling documents are ready."

"And you trust that person to be honest because I have heard many cases of fraud especially around that Lagos area."

"Eheee... I thought about that initially, but since he was a senior colleague and has helped many people, I erased my doubts. Besides, he is partly helping me financially."

"Ok. If you say so."

"Yes, papa."

"What about this girl you mentioned, are you going to tell me more about her?"

"Her name is Ifeoma. She is from a good Catholic family of Mr. and Mrs. A. N. Ugwu. She hails from Umuezeudo town. Papa, I have always seen her as a girl I will marry, but the reason why it is this sudden is that I will not like to lose her to someone else when I travel. I truly want to marry her now," he pleaded.

"Where in Umuezeudo?"

"Emete village papa."

"Alright son, I have heard all you have said. Can we have some sleep while I think about the best way to handle things?" He left for his bedroom.

"Thank you, papa." Ikedinachi felt like a huge burden has been lifted off him. He lacked words to describe how he felt. It was less diplomatic like he had imagined, far from his speculation.

Mrs. Okoro was still awake hoping to meddle when necessary but did not see any need for that rather she got more meaningful information.

"Nkem, what do you have to say about what Ikedi has just told you?" She sat on the bed.

"Well, he is a man now and is doing well. All he needs is our support. Like I told him, I need to get some sleep now and would reason better afterwards. I am tired now."

"Let's sleep," and he pulled her to the bed.

"Ok my husband, if you say so. Who am I to argue?"

Ikedinachi was marvelled on the success of his meeting with his father and thought his mother was actually more difficult. He knew that with his father's full support, it means he had nothing to worry about. He knew his mother would soon turn to him.

Maybe his mother's bitterness was about being disappointed over the so-called 'mama Ndidiamaka' and her daughter.

"No such thing will happen, over my dead body," he though out loud and shook his head in disbelief.

What indeed made his mother think that she would have control over his choices in life for such a long time beats his imaginations. He couldn't believe that she had planned to take him to Mama Ndidiamaka and her people in the next two months during Christmas. He found it extremely ridiculous.

# Ten

**Mr.** Okoro had allowed some days to go by before getting back to his son. He had thought intensely about every bit of their discussion but what disturbed him was the fact that his son said his colleague who practically is behind all of these is equally helping him out financially.

"Could he be a good Samaritan, or could there be some evil plot that is yet to befall my son?"

"No," he shook his head, "not to anyone in my household. The God of Abraham and that of our forefathers will not allow that happen to us. I still believe in miracles and have never thought or planned evil for another."

He inquired from people he knew around Umuezeudo about Ugwu's family and got vague information which made him to send some delegates. He recalled that Umuezeudo village hosted some missionaries in the early days of the church. From what he gathered, Mr. and Mrs. A.N. Ugwu had seven children, fend for all of them, and are of Catholic background. Ifeoma is their first child. He was pleased with that.

He had told his son all he needed to tell him in regards to marriage and his future, *what a father needs to tell his son*, he thought.

Having discussed properly with his wife and Ikedinachi, they all now have to prepare for what seems to be a huge task that awaits them.

Mrs. Okoro became compassionate to Ikedinachi as usual. She had to, because she observed her son virtually avoided her. They no longer sit together and chat due to the way she had tried to talk him off Ifeoma. She has never seen him behave the way he behaved lately towards her as though he was counting down the days to disappear for good.

She realised that she needed to put her son first and give him the support he so much desires from her. Her whole ranting of mama Ndidiamaka was because she thought well of him and wished he could have the best wife, if anything like that exists. She perceived Ndidiamaka as a very good girl, but since her son had gotten someone for himself, she had to let go and would find a way to explain things to mama Ndidiamaka. Her son's happiness meant a lot to her, and she would like to have her cheerful son back. And now that there is so much that is needed to be done, they need to communicate well. He used to confide in her.

Ikedinachi, his father with two of his uncles set out to Ifeoma's village. Ikedinachi and Ifeoma had previously discussed how things are done in her culture.

Things went well as planned. Ifeoma agreed that she knew who the young man was and would accept his hand in marriage and her father accepted the drink that they brought along. Mr. Ugwu traditionally welcomed Mr. Okoro into his family, and they both exchanged pleasantries. Mr. Okoro and his son made their plan of abrupt marriage known to them and after some minutes of arguments, their in-laws conceded. Of course, the issue has been discussed severally, the family investigated, and an answer agreed upon even before their arrival.

Ifeoma was contented with her parents' support as they were happy for her and already knew she would never let them down although her father frowned at the idea that Ikedinachi would be travelling so soon. Her mother saw nothing wrong with that as it implied her daughter would be leaving the country sooner or later for abroad to join her husband. That meant that her *omugwo* would be in overseas, which was the most interesting part for her. *Omugwo* is a common tradition among Nigerian mothers especially of *Igbo* extraction whereby they visit their child who had just given birth to assist with infant care for the babies first few months of life. They do prepare some special herbs and yam for the new mother to eat; which is for nourishment and cleansing purposes.

Mr. and Mrs. Okoro started making the necessary preparations. They had agreed on the traditional wedding taking place in a fortnight and had chosen *Afo*r market day while the Church wedding holds a week later in Enugu.

Ifeoma had enough running around to do. She tried to invite some of her friends within reach and had drafted a letter for Cassandra. In the letter, she told her the dates of the traditional and white wedding and encouraged her to come for the Church wedding, if she must choose one. She thought that would be the best option for her, although she gave her the directions to her hometown. She headed to the park to send the letter across to her like they planned. Sending it that way meant it would arrive on time as it takes about fourth-eight hours unlike post mail that takes couple of days or even weeks to reach to its recipients.

In the Apama park, she spent minutes searching 'Onyeije motors' as there were numerous vehicles until she asked someone who directed her to the section she had to be. When she got there, she went straight to a driver she saw at the steering of one of the vehicles.

Handing out the letter and saying, "Good morning" she told him to deliver it along with the goods that would be sent off to Alaba market in Lagos that in that way it would get to the recipient. The man had been busy admiring her in her green flowered v-neck sleeveless gown. He knew it would have been better if she had at least bothered asking him his destination before delivering her message, but he did not feel irritated by listening to her because of her initial pleasant greeting. Her voice and curvy looks had brightened his morning, and he wanted more.

"What is his name?" he asked carelessly, not willing to collect the letter.

"Don't worry about the details just send it along with other goods and it will get across."

"This girl, I need to know what is written on it. You want me to collect it, and you cannot simply tell me what is written on it." He turned away from her and started talking to one of the conductors.

"I am sorry. Please, it bears Mr. Onyema Ndu. He is a known Igbo businessman in Alaba market. The letter is for my best friend who is his wife."

"Letter for your friend? Who do you want to deceive with that story? So, you do not know your friend's postal address or cannot find your way to the post office?"

"What?" she asked. She knew she did not owe the young man explanations and was not finding the conversation useful from the way it was going and decided to go and talk to another person.

"What is your name?" the driver asked her. He had jumped down from his car and ran up to her.

"Please leave me alone, I beg of you." She struggled to let herself off the grip, but could not, instead they walked side by side.

"I thought you liked my..." he added.

"I can see that something is wrong with you. Why would anyone leave their house this early in the morning to come to the park to like a man? I am not that kind of girl."

She stopped and pulled her hand by force. If only his grip would let her off. People were staring at them.

"*He is very big o* and will give you anything you want. *Any way you want am*. Hold him *wella*. This your gown *self* needs not to be taken off. *Sharp sharp*," one of the numerous bus conductors added and onlookers laughed.

Ifeoma felt very bitter on hearing the filthy words the conductor used in referring to her. He was holding her, and her hand was placed on top of his to take it off from hers. People might have translated what they saw differently.

She had come early enough to make sure the message got to her friend as soon as it could, and she had spent roughly two hours and yet to achieve anything. She felt a sudden rush of tears in her eyes and begged him to let go of her.

"Ok. I will leave you but am willing to help you now. In fact, my bus is going to Kastina." He loosened his grip and let her off.

"Why didn't you tell me earlier? You have succeeded in wasting my time."

"I will take you to the information desk where we can get useful information regarding Lagos bus that conveys goods to Lagos." He pointed left and led the way. Ifeoma followed him because she found him reasonable now. Not that she has much options anyway.

At the information desk, they had to wait for about 20 minutes to be attended to. The driver had wanted to hasten things but was told to give them few minutes to attend to other customers since he already told them they weren't travelling.

It eventually got to their turn the old man there told them the next available bus for goods going to Lagos would be leaving the next day and made Ifeoma understand that they could guarantee her letter being conveyed to Alaba market in Lagos alongside other goods, but couldn't ascertain it gets to the right person. They had searched in their list and had found no regular customer with such name. To show how concerned he truly was, he equally searched in another list that he would not have checked ordinarily and still no hope.

"Do you know the other name of your boyfriend, maybe nickname or the name of his business?" the customer service personnel asked from the counter.

"No Sir. He is the husband of my best friend and not my boyfriend."

"That is what most of you always say. Then why are you writing to him?"

"It was my friend's idea; she said that was the only way I can get a message to her very quickly."

"You ladies usually have already made lies... as you can see, I have done my best. We do not have such name on any of our lists."

Ifeoma shook her head on the kind of people she met that morning. Maybe, it was the way they see all girls, or it had to do with the nature of their job and where they find themselves. She sighed in dismay.

They were convinced he must have been using a nickname or definitely a different name for his business like many other traders. Ifeoma still pleaded he packed them along with those goods and begged him to speak with the bus driver on her behalf. He agreed and showed her the driver in case she wanted to talk to him too.

She walked to the man and explained everything to him, and he promised to do his best to ensure her envelope got to the desired recipient and did not beat about the bush like others. She was fulfilled at last.

Her bus driver companion has been on and off. She thanked him for helping her out after all. He had been hanging around and was glad that he can now discuss business.

"You are going to spend some time with me before you go *nah?*. You know I have waited for you all these while," he winked at her. As he didn't get a similar response or anything near that back, he pleaded.

"I sincerely appreciate. But I have to go. I didn't know I would be staying this long." The sun was up already, she had not eaten and was very tired; tired from the stress of finding the right bus or too much talking, she couldn't tell. They all sure contributed to it.

"When is your bus supposed to leave?" she asked wondering whether he was not traveling to Katsina again.

The bus-driver had fantasized having her in his arms and caressing all parts of her body, one after another and doing all sorts of things with her in any secluded place be it in an isolated vehicle or in a shed. He was gravely disappointed by her response. His mood changed, which reflected in his tone.

"I was not the one to drive the bus today. I was only checking it before you walked up to me. You do not think I am that stupid to abandon my bus and follow you around the park. Were you told I have never seen a woman before? What do you have that I have not seen or touched?"

Ifeoma noticed his odd tone. Knowing that the discussion was sounding rather awkward, she took to her heels.

At home, she was exhausted and could not carry out all she had intended for the day. Mere taking a letter to the park took so much time but she was delighted it was a success after all she had encountered. Later that day, she narrated the experience to her mother and siblings, and they all laughed at her. Her mother told her not to worry about that as it was how most guys in the motor park behave.

The next couple of days were filled more with events such as going to market and putting things in order as they prepared to travel to Umuezeudo, their hometown by the weekend.

In the village, Mr. Ugwu had formally contacted the elders to make them aware of his daughter's forthcoming marriage and to carry out the necessary rites as expected of him by his community. He had informed his in-laws what were required from them and where his own family would come in.

He had agreed with his wife to see to the upkeep of the traditional marriage since it takes place in his house. Mr. Okoro was glad to hear that when he told him about their contribution. It would earn him some respect from his in-laws.

# Eleven

**As** events began to unfold, Ikedinachi became more aware of the demands that were yet to be met. The traditional marriage list they had collected from Mr. Ugwu would rip them off a huge sum of money. Despite the fact that their in-laws offered to provide for the traditional marriage, the list still contained items like bushels of rice, tubers of yam, various meat, and many other foodstuffs, including cartons of drinks and gallons of palmwine, which are likely to be used on that very day. It was obvious that they were the ones virtually doing everything although, they could not tell what was left that Mr. and Mrs. Ugwu would be helping with. He shook his head and tried not to let the contents of the list worry him much and simply do what he needed to do.

Ikedinachi discussed with his father about the things that needed to be done and he told him that he would take care of the drinks and that he should meet his mother to discuss about the kind of food items and meat that could be gotten from their farmland. Ikedinachi was pleased with the efforts of his supportive family because they made things much easier for him.

The special day was fast approaching, and Mrs. Okoro had able to provide many items from the farm. Everybody in the family saw to the progress of the wedding preparation. Ugonna helped with errands while Adanna carried out some petty tasks at home.

Ikedinachi recollected things that needed immediate attention while sitting on the veranda. Obinna pushed the gate open and walked in. He was told by his Mother that Ikedinachi was in town. He was surprised that he had not cared to stop by. The next day, after work, he went to see him as they had not seen in a while.

"Obinna!!!" Ikedinachi shouted and reached out to him. "Please forgive your brother. I have extremely busy and have delayed visiting you for so long now. How are you?"

"I am good Ike. Was wondering why you have refused to check on me since you came in. Anyway, how is life?"

"Life has been treating your friend well. I knew that I should have been to your place," he robbed the back of his head. "Forgive your brother"

Obinna approached him and they hugged. "Well you know what they say, if Mohammed doesn't go to the mountain, the mountain will come to him."

"Obi, your guy has been very busy. Please come inside." Ikedinachi sent off Ugonna to buy some drinks for them. They enjoyed their drink while they had a long chat that they had both longed for.

"Long time Obyno!"

"Yes. Long-time indeed. That's life after school for you. How is Lagos?"

"Lagos is okay. I have been running around for so many things lately. By the way, how is work and your family?" They left the parlour where they sat to the veranda as it became hot for them. Besides, there was no power supply.

"We are all fine. Work can be stressful sometimes. It was my mother that told me you are around. I occasionally do run into your parents and siblings."

"That's good. I have concluded plans with regards to travelling abroad, and I intend to travel soon which entails I marry Ifeoma before leaving."

He concisely narrated all he had done and those he intends to do to Obinna.

"I would have come to your house to inform you, but I've have been battling with time and have succumbed to delaying paying you a visit."

"You have been very occupied my guy. That's good news Ikedi. I am thrilled about you and Ifeoma, you both have come a long way. I wish I can help. Don't hesitate to call on me when necessary. I am happy that you have finally succeeded with your travel plan. I remember clearly how frustrated you felt back then in school."

"How is Ifeoma?" Obinna asked wanting to know how well everything has gone and where he can fit in.

"She is doing well. We were in her hometown throughout yesterday trying to finalise plans. I will be coming over to your place tomorrow to invite your parents. It is not easy to be a man Obyno. Sometimes, things seem so easy to imagine but very tedious to carry out," he sighed.

"You are right. I trust you, I know you can handle anything. You are going to be fine," he reassured his friend.

"That's it. Hope you are still with Cynthia?"

"Sure, we are fine. I have been making some enquiries about going for my masters. Although I am going to let a few years pass by before I delve into it."

"I see. That's great. You are a very focused person. Acada himself!" *Acada being what their peers would call someone with much academic acquisition.*

"You are not like me, that is filled with crazy ideas," he laughed.

"Who said so? Not at all. I think we are both doing well for ourselves and that's what matters."

"Yes, yes... I guess you are right."

Obinna was excited for his friend. He remembered how Ikedinachi had been so sad and depressed in their university days when he had gone to inquire about Emeka – the-abroad-connection-guy, and was told he never existed.

Apparently, Ekaette was replaced with Itorobong, and no one was able to identify Emeka or match any person to Ikedinachi's description of Emeka. He would go there from time to time hoping that either Emeka or Ekaette would appear. He thought about them and dreamt about them.

Each time, he would begin to describe Emeka thinking maybe, there was something in the description he was not getting right. It got to the point that he started sounding like a broken record and Itorobong's madam did not find his visit funny any longer.

The first time, they spared him some time but did not pay further attention to him on subsequent visits. Worst still, he could not tell them why exactly he was looking for someone whom they did not to know.

"*He owe you money?*" Itorobong had asked.

"No... no at all. I just need to see him," Ikedinachi responded.

"*You sabi any of him friends? Maybe, they fit help.*"

"No"

Normally, he would not eat from that very canteen, but he chose to patronise them regularly till Obinna was able to talk him off it. He acted like he had lost something very significant to him. It took weeks for Obinna to reassure and bring him back to normalcy. Obinna made him realise he had not made any commitment to Emeka and should move on.

"Better opportunities lie ahead," Obinna told his friend on one occasion. They both laughed hard as they recalled the encounter.

"You were right Obi about the better opportunities. Thanks mate for your support all these times." They shook hands.

"Anytime. I'm very happy for you. I will be leaving now, see you tomorrow then." Obinna stood up and stretched himself. Coincidentally, Obinna was able to meet Ikedinachi's parents. Mr. Okoro had just arrived from work while Mrs. Okoro who has been out to visit a customer who has been owing her for a long time, got home too.

"Good evening sir! Good evening ma," Obinna greeted them.

"Good evening papa," Ikedinachi welcomed his father and carried his briefcase which he sent into the house and joined his friend.

"How are you Obinna? And your people?"

"We are fine sir."

"Hope my arrival is not making you leave?" Mr. Okoro asked.

"No Sir, I was on my way before you both came in. I have stayed for so long."

"Mmm... Obinna," he cleared his throat. "Please, tell your father that I shall come over to see him on Saturday evening."

"Ok sir. Your message will reach him the moment I get home."

"Obinna, hope you are good?" Mrs. Okoro exchanged greetings with them and went off to the kitchen to prepare dinner.

"Yes ma."

"You have done so well Obyno. I will be in your place tomorrow in the evening." Ikedinachi saw him off, almost close to his house.

"Nkem, how was work today?" Mrs. Okoro asked her husband.

"It went well as usual… I am very tired." He yawned and reclined on the sofa. "And sales?"

"Little by little my dear. I was lucky enough to meet Mrs. Opara today while I was going to see that woman that I told you that said that the money she has owed me for a long time will be ready today. I told her about our son's wedding and told her that we would still come over to her place to invite her and her husband properly."

She served dinner which they both ate while their chat continued.

"Oh, that's nice! There are still many people to invite, keep informing those you come by. It is not everyone that I would make out time to visit," Mr Okoro added.

"That's true. I would because I will like my son's wedding to be amongst the best in town."

"Eheee… that woman was able to pay me after chanting the litanies of her problem. I felt for her, but I need money now and had to collect it. I'm glad she was able to pay up this particular time. I invited her too, and she promised to attend the white wedding and said that she would not make it to Umuezeudo village as she has an important engagement that day."

"I have gone for the drinks like I promised Ikedi. I have paid for them too."

"Thank you dim oma," she rubbed his back and smiled.

"Adanna!" Mr. Okoro called out.

"Yes, papa." She went and sat beside him, and he gave her the piece of meat that he had kept for her. He loves his daughter and likes keeping meat or fish for her most times.

"How was school today?"

"I was hungry after school. I only ate puff-puff at break time."

"Obidiya, please do make sure she has enough snacks all the time. After eating, go inside and get my glass case on the table."

"Oh! You and your daughter! Adannaya, are you not supposed to be hungry after school? You simply come home and eat."

"Nkem, this meat you are giving her all the time is becoming too much. You are spoiling her."

"Obidiya, nothing is wrong with that."

Adanna happily ate the meat and licked up the remaining soup. She helped her mother to clear the table and rushed off to get her father's case knowing what would come next. When she got back, her father collected the case from her and gave her ten naira. She happily jumped out of the palour.

"Adanna, do not spend all that money in school tomorrow."

"Yes, ma," she shouted from the room.

# Twelve

**Ifeoma** began to feel the heat of the whole activities. Initially, she thought that sorting out various clothings for different groups would be so much fun, but there was more to that. Her mother helped her by choosing *mkpuru-oka* and *kirikiri-star* for the women while she went for a red and blue *abada* for her mates.

Her age grade members eventually agreed on a particular style for their clothes after several deliberations and arguments, at the end, she was pleased with what they came up with.

"Ify, what about the kind of sandals we are going to wear, or have you made some preparations for us?" one of the girls asked.

"No Nne, not really," she was yet to provide any meaningful answer before another person interrupted her.

"I thought it would be better if we all wear beads around our waist, hands, and legs. Are the sandals necessary?"

"Please shut up!" "Close your mouth if you do not know what to say please."

"What?"

"We are going to wear sandal, if you want to go barefoot, wait for some other event," she hissed.

"It was only a suggestion, you all should not eat me up. Haba!"

Ifeoma called upon the head girl to calm her girls down because they were beginning to make the meeting difficult by having biased ideas and throwing insults to each other. She observed that some see themselves as the big babes and see others as minors and it affected how they communicate ideas. She excused herself for some minutes and left them.

They later agreed to wear shiny rubber sandals with beads a little above their ankles. Putting on that trendy footwear would make the guys in the village know that they have class and are no longer kids.

Amongst the folk songs they usually present, they have a favourite and after much talk, they chose to display their latest dance steps. Some of them would have preferred to learn a new song, but since they did not have enough time before the wedding, they succumbed to the opinion of others.

Their leader and her clique demonstrated and moved their legs as if they were already wearing their new pair of sandals.

She called upon all to do a brief rehearsal to ensure they still know the songs very well and then make some necessary modifications where required.

They started singing and clapping as thus:

*Akpukpu ukwu anyi na-agba na kolota*
*Sanwa sanwa*
*Orugo mgbe anyi ji eme iyanga*
*O o o o ya*
*O o o o onye okwere omume*
*Sanwa sanwa....*

They sang happily, whined their waists, and swinged their hands while hitting their feet hard on the ground in synchrony. It was obvious that their folk dance on that day would be exceedingly entertaining.

Watching the girls reminded Ifeoma of her childhood days. While they were little, they looked forward to festive periods such as Christmas and new yam festivals. Each year, they would learn new dance steps and add to the ones they already knew. They were beautiful to watch. Who wouldn't want to see beautiful little cuties displaying their dance moves? They would dance from house to house, in occasions, and in the market squares too. The villagers always come out on hearing the whistle of their head girl to watch them. Her age grade girls were one of the best dancers in their time and were very popular as a result.

For some weird reasons, it was assumed in their village that when you have danced, you become popular and cannot hide anymore. You would be expected to be of a very good conduct, as though dancing had a connection with morality. The things you see in Umuezeudo village.

One thing all the little girls looked forward to was the aspect of sharing the money at the end. It meant they made money for themselves whilst enjoying themselves and entertaining their people. It gained them lots of admirers too. It was a norm in Umuezeudo for their girls to be spotted from dance and saved for marriage.

Ifeoma re-joined them and was pleased that they had sorted out their differences and agreed on a particular idea. She inquired from them if there were other things required from her apart from the usual stuffs which she is fully aware of. Earlier, her mother had bought a crate of mineral drink and a packet of cabin biscuit which was sent across to them as a means of invitation.

She was told nothing else was remaining, but they were willing to accept any gift she wishes to support them with.

"Well, I will give you some money to add to the purchase of the sandals. Is that ok?" she asked in a mild tone.

"Yes of course!" They were all pleased. They starred and tapped each other too. She just surprised them.

She opened her purse and handed out some money to their leader and made them understand that she appreciated the fact that they were willing to make her day very special despite the urgency. Her family passion for education and her personal achievement so far made her highly rated among her age grade members. They were exhilarated and could not conceal how they felt. They promised to get everything ready before the big day.

As for their hairstyle and decoration, they settled for stylish cornrows and single plaits; the type that they would be able to part and knot nicely with red ribbons. They would beautify their faces with eye pencil drawings. The head-girl and two other girls volunteered to go to the market within the next two days for the sandals and other stuffs they needed, which they agreed should be sent across latest on the evening of the next *Eke* market day when they would be gathering again. This was essential in order to ensure that sandals fit each of them very well.

Eventually, they ended their meeting. They dispersed in pairs discussing the outcome of their gathering and looking forward to all necessary preparations and the main day.

Ifeoma's siblings were all involved in the preparations too. Her immediate younger sister Chinenye took all of her siblings- Obiageli, Uchechi, Izuchukwu, Chukwudi, and Onyeka to the tailor's shop in Owerre before they came home. Things went like they had wished. On collection of the clothes, the tailors who usually disappoints her customers, fortunately, made sure their clothes were almost ready for collection.

Although, the girls' clothes were displayed and ready for collection, she waited a little bit for Izuchukwu, Chukwudi, and Onyeka's clothes to be neatly trimmed and ironed. Setting the charcoal iron alight took a great deal of time, but it was worth the wait after all. She was of the opinion that all are part of the charge and shouldn't be overlooked. Despite availability of electricity, many tailors still rely on the good old charcoal iron, Chinenye wondered why.

When she got home, they all tried their clothes one after the other and it fitted them quite well. They were almost set for their eldest sister's day. Mrs. Ugwu's mind was at least at rest knowing that her kids were sorted out cloth-wise. It was remaining hers and that of her husband which would be ready for collection the next day following the postponement they encountered the previous day. She was pissed off that very day but had to go home and attend to other things hoping she does not experience that the next time. Her tailor apologised to her and told her that they had bulk of work lately, but she was going to leave out some and attend to hers since she is a regular customer and would not like to lose her to some other tailors.

Ifeoma shuttled between Umuezeudo and Enugu to ensure that nothing was been left out.

Mr. Ugwu was able to do some renovations in his bungalow and repainted it too. He wanted the marriage of his first daughter to be a special one and did the best he could not minding the limited time available. He had discussed with his wife about the necessary things and help that they could require. He had already contacted men of his age grade and they had started clearing the bushy pathway that lead to his compound although with the help of some youths too.

His wife and other women of the kindred fetched firewood and made plans about cooking for that day. Some women agreed to come a day before the day of occasion to help with cooking while others would join them very early in the morning. They agreed to boil the meats and make stew which can easily be made into jollof rice the next morning. They had organised themselves as they seem to know each other well as the have done this severally in the past and therefore could tell what each other was capable of and what they were best at.

Thanks to the underground tank in Mr. Ugwu's compounds, water would have posed a big problem, but the kids still need to go the stream to get portable water that is safe for drinking.

Umuezeudo village is popularly known for its sparkling spring water which attracts lots of people from other villages and neighbouring towns. It is usually cool and tasteless. According to the villagers, it has that kind of quality that would not let one put the cup down till the last drop is gulped. As a result, most locals already know when they are given a different water and simply term the rest as unsafe for drinking.

At the Ngene stream, there is a particular spot where the spring water gushes out from rocks, and that is where indigenes usually collect the best water. Water that collects underneath makes up the stream and is used for cooking, bathing, and washing.

Mr. and Mrs. Ugwu's compound had taken a different look within the last few days.

# Thirteen

**The** day Ifeoma had long waited for had eventually drawn close. It was only a night away. Inasmuch as they all thought they were going to have some time to rest and look a bit fresh for the day, it seemed that they were all going to keep running around till the whole event comes to an end.

It was dry season, and only a few canopies were mounted as luck was on their side. Rain rarely fell around that time of the year. The neighbours could sense the festive moods. Most of their relatives were around and helping as well. Mrs. Ugwu's sisters had come to spend the night and help her out with cooking, washing, and tidying up as well.

"Where are they?" Mrs. Ugwu's immediate younger sister called out as she walked into the compound with lots of heavy bags. The Okada man that dropped her had left. Ordinarily, someone would have heard the horn by the bike man and should have ran out, but it did not happen due to the noisy festive atmosphere.

"Aunty! Aunty!" the kids shouted and rushed towards her. They all wanted to hug her at the same time.

"Oby, Izu, Uchee, Onyi.... who do I call and who do I leave out? How are you all doing?" She handed out a nylon containing biscuits and bread to them.

"We are fine, aunty." They collected the bags she was carrying and headed inside the house.

"There is another bag over there too," she pointed to the bag she left behind.

Chukwudi and Uchechi managed to carry the heavy bag inside the house.

"Aunty, what of Ujunwa and Chidiebube?" Obiageli asked.

"Uju was supposed to come along with me, but her father needs her, don't worry they will all be here tomorrow."

Ifeoma and her mother were happy to see her because they were worried about her late arrival as the roads were bad, and anything could go wrong.

"Mama Uju! Hey! Look at you... you are still putting on more weight? Your husband is really doing so much work on you."

"Yes of course! Is it water that I have been drinking to get to this size?"

They were all amused. She greeted and hugged her sisters and in-laws.

'Please come and have a seat after this long journey," Mrs. Ugwu added.

"What about your family? I thought your handbag-*Uju* would have come with you?"

"My dear, they will all be here tomorrow with their father. There is no need asking you how things are; I can see things are going well. I will need to change my clothes to see what I can start with."

"Ok dear, we need to get things going as fast as we can."

"Aunty, welcome. I have missed you so much." Ifeoma ran into her arms.

"Mama, you are lucky all your siblings are here tonight. We have a full house." She loves her aunts so much and usually enjoys their company.

"Ify my baby is getting married. You look ravishing like your mother while she was in her youth." Ifeoma giggled. She had already plaited her afro hair and looked elegantly beautiful. It was as though she had been totally transformed within the last few days.

"Madam the madam!"

*"Oji ego na ekwu!"* meaning 'It is the matter of cash.' Mama Uju responded while raising her shoulders high as though she was in a parade. She liked being praised for her looks. She is not the boastful type but very cheerful and generous. Well, that's the kind of feeling she has when in the company of her loving siblings. It sure brings good childhood memories to them all. Her husband is not that rich, but she is very comfortable in her marital home.

It is always fun when they gather together for the festive seasons or special events like this one. She changed into a casual wear and joined them as they chatted, ate, and did lots of works together. That way, they were able to achieve more. They equally enjoyed the light from the generator which also attracted more helpers from the neighbourhood and enabled them stay awake for so long. Kids who were still awake took it to be a play time. It was indeed a lovely atmosphere. Mrs. Ugwu had purchased two additional lanterns to the ones they already had and about three *mpanaka* which saw them through when her husband turned off the generator set.

However, other women resolved to locally made palm-stick that glows when lighted- *Akpuru-akpu*. It is prepared by heaping chunks of molten seedless palm kernel fibre on a stick and allowing it to dry up. It is being used for various purposes like setting up fire while cooking with tripod stand and for outdoor lightening up in darkness at night. It was popularly known and used by indigenes of Umuezeudo village. Therefore, Mrs. Ugwu packed lots of them knowing they could be of much help as they cannot afford to run out.

Later that night most of their visitors and helpers began squeezing themselves onto beds and mats for the night rest and sleep, and gradually they all retired for the day although most of them would have to wake up early in the morning to commence further cooking.

Elsewhere in Enugu town, Ikedinachi and his father had painstakingly done all the running around required. Mr. Okoro had scheduled with the local Achafu *Igba* dancers to accompany him to his in-laws, and, he was able to charter a minibus that would convey some of his guests. With some drinks available too, they were almost ready to bring their wife home.

Obinna and his family were one of their main guests, and he made a special cloth for his friend's marriage ceremony. He had planned to attend with Cynthia, but as it was not convenient for her, he would be attending with his family, which was equally good as he did not want his parents to know his whereabouts with women till the day he tells them to escort him to his would-be in-law's house for introduction rites. With that in his mind, he focused on attending and being very supportive of his friend in any way that he could. He did spend the last couple of evenings with him whenever he was back from work. Although most of their chat had been more of the impending church wedding, they could not wait for the traditional aspect to come and go.

Mrs. Okoro made some preparation for the reception of her daughter-in-law. She and her friends prepared some dishes for the guests that would be accompanying them to their in-laws. Her friend, mama Ndidiamaka would have been around if not for the argument they had some days back over the fact that she accused her of deceiving her into believing that her son would marry her daughter. She did not let that trouble her because her siblings and in-laws were of much help.

# Fourteen

**The** long-awaited day has eventually come. There were variety of dishes, ranging from jollof rice, pounded yam and *egusi* soup, assorted meats, to *abach*a decorated with fishes and garden eggs.

Mr. Ugwu sent out his junior brother to the market to fetch kegs of palm-wine and nkwu-enu. He made other drinks available as well.

Ifeoma was adorned by her mates. They neatly and stylishly decorated her plaited afro hair with assorted beads. She wore beads around her waist, hands, and on her ankles too. They did some artistic drawings with eye pencils on her face which made her look like a princess.

Her age grade girls looked stunning too. Just like every other person, her siblings were all dressed up lovely in their uniform attire.

The woman in-charge of decorating the entire compound did a great job with her girls. They beautified the canopies and mounted a pole in the centre of the compound, and linked banners to various parts of the building. They made sure they incorporated vibrant colours like red, green, and golden to illuminate the whole place. Besides, they were among the colours Ifeoma had chosen for herself,

Ikedinachi, and her girls. Flamboyant buntings in blue and red colours scattered all over the compound.

They showed the craftiness of their work on how they laid the seats for Ifeoma and Ikedinachi in the bride and groom corner where they used clothes of various thickness and quality. They also helped Ifeoma with some accessories like raffia hand-fan and extra beads.

Ikedinachi in his majesty, accompanied by family and friends arrived at 3.15 pm to his in-law's compound. It was his day, and so the event kicked off upon their arrival.

They were ushered in by the sounds of the magnificent drums and whistles of the *Umu Achafu* local dancers. Ikedinachi's entourage was indeed great. Ikedinachi's regalia was very captivating.

He walked majestically while his followers all danced as they headed towards the canopy that was reserved for them.

Onlookers were pleased with their entertainment, and most of them were busy assessing and admiring Ifeoma's husband.

"He must be rich. Ifeoma is very lucky," one of the girls uttered.

The master of the ceremony for the day announced the arrival of their special in-laws, and after some moments the elders amongst them including Ikedinachi and his father were all called inside the parlour for important discussion and negotiations.

There were so many attendees amongst them who were special guests from Enugu and Owerre. They were welcomed during this time and given special seats.

It took them a while to sort out the differences, which was not strange. Usually, when a woman is leaving her parent's house, the talk is not always that easy. They eventually concluded well and came out smiling while some were still chatting and whispering to each other.

In the company of her age grade girls, Ifeoma came and greeted her in-laws and visitors. Dancing and smiling joyously, she paraded around her guests.

Later, she came out the second time, when she searched for her husband with a palm-wine in her hand. She found Ikedinachi, and he drank the wine, which signified that he is truly the one. She then took him to her parents. They both knelt before Mr. and Mrs. Ugwu for their blessings. The MC then handed the microphone over to Mr. Ugwu.

He blessed them and wished them good health, long life, many children just like themselves.

"Obedience to your husband and an undying love for one another."

"Ifeoma my daughter, always remember that you came from a good home and build your new home in God. We always have you in mind and do not forget us your parents and your siblings."

As he spoke, Ifeoma felt very emotional as though she suddenly realised she was going to leave them. Ikedinachi grabbed her right hand and squeezed it tightly, in a manner that shows love and affection.

"Ify, Adannaya, your father has said it all. Be a good wife to your husband."

Later, they were joined by friends as they both danced happily and enjoyed their day. Their DJ chose a fitting song *'Adanma ribe ife'* by Thompson Oranu. It has been a great day for them and marked the beginning of their new life together.

The age grade girls paraded themselves so well and were able to get some admirers too. They displayed their special dance, and all looked adoring in their colourful outfits and sandals.

Both families were very pleased with each other, the ceremony went well, and food and drinks were plenty for their guests.

Her parents presented the gifts they bought for her which included household items such as three different sizes of mortar and pestle, big black frying pan, big yellow food warmer, big pans and stainless washing-hand basins, baby bathing sets among other numerous items. It was their first child's wedding, and they were very proud of whom she has become. Ifeoma never expected that much from them because of the urgency of the preparation yet they made her so proud.

Ifeoma had already picked few of her belongings and packed them in a little new box she purchased in Lagos. She struggled to hold back tears while she hugged her parents, siblings, and relatives as she went home with her husband in the company of her kid sister Chinenye like their tradition holds.

As their car sped off, they were still hearing the song that the DJ was playing. This time he chose to play the *'The anyi n'emere onwe anyi'* track. The lyrics filled Ifeoma's ears. Most of the songs played were appropriate for all the various sections of the occasion.

They got home late and were all tired and worn out. It had been a very hectic but wonderful day for them. Their neighbours found the whole occasion thrilling and a memorable one.

The next couple of days, Mr. and Mrs. Okoro hosted lots of visitors as they came to see and welcome the new wife.

Ifeoma was delighted with her new home and in-laws too. Mr. Okoro and his wife were nice people, and both loved her. Ikedinachi's mother made her comfortable and made her understand that she was unreservedly welcomed into the family.

For Ifeoma, it was truly a good sign for a new beginning. She had always been assured of Ikedinachi's love for her but could not tell much about his parents, but now she is so pleased with the kind of people she perceived they are.

*What more can a daughter-in-law ask for?* she imagined. She bonded well with Adanna.

Chinenye equally enjoyed her little stay. However, on the third day after the traditional marriage, Ifeoma visited her parents according to their tradition. This is usually done in Umuezeudo village to enable their daughters to give feedback about their new home. In addition, they are expected to return soonest to ensure everything had gone well as expected.

On her arrival at her parent's house, she was welcomed like they had not seen her in a very long time. Her mother was of a stronger opinion that she had already put on some weight while her Obiageli teased her about looking more beautiful. She could not help but keep smiling and wondered how they happened to see things so quickly and under the space of three days.

She had a nice time with her mother telling her about the lovely reception she got from Ikedinachi's parents and how she felt so much that their future was going to be very bright.

Mr. Ugwu thanked God for her daughter and prayed that the happiness she had found would remain with her till eternity. Amidst this, he reminded himself of the church wedding that would be taking place the coming weekend. He was a little bit relieved as it would not take place in his compound and would not be that stressful for them this time around.

He started making the necessary arrangements for another wedding, but they were lucky that most of their guests were previously informed. All they needed to do was to make an arrangement on how they would be conveyed to Enugu on that very day.

At Enugu, Ikedinachi and his best man, Obinna got themselves a black suit and new pairs of shoes. Obinna was very supportive of his friend and ensured he made himself available as often as he can. It was only a week to Ikedinachi's church wedding, and they planned as much as they could despite Ikedinachi not wanting it to be an elaborate one. He was cutting down on expenses to enable him to spare some money for his travel.

On Friday night, Ikedinachi narrated to his parents how he had successfully finalised his meeting with Fr. John, the parish priest of St. Mary's Church. Ikedinachi and Ifeoma had previously met him for their marriage preparation and had fulfilled what was required of them. It was not their local church, but it was his parent's idea that he weds there as it was a magnificent church with lots of paintings and beautifications that depicts the Catholic church in its glorious splendour when compared to their home parish St. Joseph's Catholic Church located in their neighbourhood.

They were all pleased with the progress that they have made so far. Ikedinachi's father could not wait for the whole event to come to pass while his mother at times was moody by pondering over the fact that all these rushes would soon end, and his son would travel to an unknown country. Nevertheless, she did not let her thoughts reflect so much on her character and tried as much as she could to conceal her feelings.

On Saturday, Ikedinachi had been able to contact some of his old schoolmates that he wanted to honour his day. He did not deem it necessary to invite any of his work colleague from Lagos and did not bother to contact any of them. He was later joined by Obinna that evening.

As they chatted and strolled on the street, they ran into Enuma, a former classmate of theirs while they were in secondary school.

"Ikedi, look at who we have here."

"Hey, this guy," Ikedinachi responded not knowing exactly how to approach him.

Enuma was few steps closer to them, and they had already seen each other. Hurriedly, Ikedinachi turned to the other side of the road to purchase some akara balls from a petty trader.

"Ma, how do you sell?"

"This side 1 naira, that side 2 naira," the woman pointed to her tray. "Which ones do you want?"

"Em... I think the 3 naira own would do."

"Obyno, how many do I get?" And he turned towards his friend who was now joined by Enuma. He heard them exchanging greeting and pretended to be busy as the area was noisy too.

"Long-time Enuma, how is life treating you?" Obinna asked him.

"Am good. You and this your cunny friend. He is pretending not to see me."

"Oh boy, how far?"

"I know you must have seen me and went off to buy akara."

*"Bia nwa a, I ma gozi mu akala?"* This boy, won't you buy my akara again?

"If not, please shift to another side. I do not want people blocking my table and others would think am selling while am not."

The woman frowned at them and sang, "Hot akara, who wants it?" as she looked for more customers. It is her usual way of attracting passers-by.

"Obi how many did you say?"

"Get two pieces for me and some that you would take home to Adanna."

"Yes, she likes it. Enuma do you want some?"

"Ikedi buy akara lets chop and stop asking questions."

Ikedinachi wanted to ask him how many he was going to eat but simply got four for him without asking.

"Do you want pepper and onions in all of them?"

"Emm... not all."

"Guys?" Ikedinachi drew their attention to the question.

Obinna said no while Enuma asked for plenty of it.

The woman wrapped the ones Ikedinachi had chosen and handed them over to him. He gave the boys their pack while they left and continued with their chat.

"Ikedi, I heard you did your traditional marriage last week and will be doing your white one next week. You don't even want to tell me about it?"

"Yes, that's true. I was about to tell you."

"You are invited to the wedding next week Saturday at St. Mary's. You will attend, right?"

"Is that how they invite someone to a wedding? If I had not mentioned it, you might not have told me about it."

"No, I would have hinted you about it," Ikedinachi uttered scratching the back of his head.

"Besides, Obinna is it not what we have been doing lately?" he sought some support from his friend.

"You are invited Enuma, come and support your guys."

"Alright! If you both say so... let's see, I might make it." He shook hands with them and went off.

Ikedinachi hissed while he left which alerted Obinna.

"Why did you do that?"

"Enuma is trouble! I simply don't know why he likes attacking me all the time. I know he was going to find what to say I have done to him, that was why I felt like not talking to him at first."

"And you went for the akara balls? Well, I think he sounds quite ok. I hope he attends though."

"He is cheeky you know?" He sighed. "Anyway, let's see. If he does, fine although, I do not think he would like to come."

As they strolled, Ikedinachi told Obinna how he was pleased that he was almost through with all that he needed to put in place for his day next week Saturday. He mentioned the fact that he had visited Fr. John on Friday to conclude his preparations.

His friend was happy to hear that and asked him if there were other things that were left to be done that he could help with.

"Nothing that much Obyno. You have been of immense help already. I do not know how I would have been able to do all these without your help. But I am going to discuss with my father to see how far he has gone with the drinks and know how they have planned to supply them on that very day. I am really lucky with the amount of support I have gotten from everyone."

"Obyno, what about Cynthia? The other time I mentioned you seemed not willing to discuss her and was keener on the wedding preparation. Please, can you talk to me now?"

He smiled quietly. "Mmm… there is not much to tell, that's why I have decided we focus on more important things. She seems to be more involved with a colleague of hers in Campus ever since we left. She still claims to love me, but I guess things are a bit different now. Well, the other day she came around I mentioned your wedding to her, and she said she would be pleased to come. So hopefully she would make it on that day too."

"Oh! I am so sorry to hear that. I know how much you loved her. I mean at times I wonder why people that seem to deserve the best usually encounter such difficulty. You are going to find someone who would stick by you at all time. So sorry bro… I can't even believe you still mentioned the wedding to her?"

"Ikedi, I'm okay. It is her choice and I'm not going to let that bother me for now. You know I am not that much into women. Of course, she is our friend that's was why I invited her. I guess she would be happy to see you and Ifeoma wed."

Their hearty chat continued as they arrived at Obinna's house. Obinna's parents and siblings were all sitting on the sofa in the palour listening to moonlight tales. It had been a routine in their house as his parents loved telling stories to them in the night right from childhood. It used to be a large family of seven- five boys and two girls, before his parents lost two boys. From infancy, they suffered unknown health conditions that presented with various signs and symptoms, which made doctors move swiftly from one diagnosis to another. The deaths shrank their number to five. At that time, they feared it would happen to their other future kids, but with luck on their side, Mr. and Mrs. Mmadu's household did not record further deaths since the last time.

"Welcome brother. Good evening."

Ogechi and Olanma, Obinna's kid sisters greeted and welcomed Ikedinachi while Ebuka simply left the parlour for the room. He was immediately followed by his younger brother, Ndukaku as though they are programmed to leave the sitting room whenever they have a guest, irrespective of the fact that Ikedinachi was not seen as a visitor in their house anymore.

Ikedinachi greeted his friend's parents who were happy for him. They asked him how he was faring regarding his forthcoming wedding and praised him for the success of the traditional one that went smoothly. Mr. and Mrs. Mmadu liked seeing their son's friend around and have admired their friendship.

He had only wanted to see his friend's family as it was obvious they were always there for him and his family most times. He told them that he would be on his way while Mrs. Mmadu had sent out Ogechi to fetch them food.

"Please stay so that you can both have dinner," she pleaded with him.

"No mama. Thank you. I will leave it for next time. I need to be home now."

"Why don't you at least drink water?"

"Olanma! Go and get your brother's friend a cup of water. It is not good that you came around and did not take anything. You can at least soothe your throat. I know you both must have been chatted for a while," she teased him.

Ikedinachi smiled as she persuaded him to at least drink some water before taking off. He drank from the cup of water that Olanma had kept on a side stool beside him. He told them that he would be expecting them the D-day, while Obinna escorted him.

To Obinna's mother, he was the kind of person that their son deserved as he usually keeps to himself much like his father.

# Fifteen

**At** Emete village in Umuezeudo, Ifeoma's parents were making the necessary preparations for the church wedding. At first, they thought that since it was not going to take place in their residence like the traditional one that they had little or nothing to worry about this time. But they were damn wrong.

Ifeoma's relatives and especially her favourite uncle, Ahubekwe who had come back from Ibadan to grace the occasion, were all in ecstatic mood and planned her church wedding in a very big way. Ifeoma is one of a kind because there were only a few academicians in their whole village and to buttress the whole fact, she was the only woman among them. They were all proud of her and wanted to play their part by being very supportive of her.

Despite their love and respect for tradition, Ugwu family is popularly known for their profound Catholic faith and the roles that their forefathers have played in the church and during the days of the White missionaries. It implied that church wedding was of more importance and cements the entire marriage process.

The women chose to wear a beautiful and exorbitant uniform of *kirikiri-star* cloth with white lace, red handbag, and red Scholl footwear to go with it.

Ahubekwe was not around during the traditional marriage. He went to Mr. Ugwu to know if there are some functions he would help with. Luckily for Mr. ugwu, he offered to pay for the vehicle that would convey their guests to Enugu and gave him some money to run other expenses. He equally bought some drinks that they would use in entertaining themselves.

In fact, throughout his stay, it was one joyful mood after another in an equally lookalike festive time. He so much liked and admired Ifeoma for her courage and persistence. His brother explained to him about the urgency of the marriage and all that revolved around it which he understood. The whole idea of Ikedinachi getting married to her and travelling abroad soonest seemed a bit dodgy or not very well clear to him, but he was of the opinion that if not for Ifeoma that is involved, he would have reasoned differently, maybe not given his approval and would not have bothered coming back.

He had the same chat with Ifeoma and was somewhat convinced that it is a very good thing and wished her luck. Despite his doubts, he loves her and did not want to make her feel bad or worried especially as it was just two days to her day. He was only being concerned.

"I understand that you are worried uncle, but we are going to be fine. I will join him in England as soon as he is settled."

"Ifeoma, life abroad can be difficult, it might not work out as you both think right now, I have few friends over there, and they do tell about their ugly encounters. Well, let us not discuss that further. I mean well."

"Thanks, uncle. I know you mean well. I have a strong feeling that we are going to be fine no matter what happens.

I will be going to join mama now because I will leave tomorrow morning to Enugu."

"Ok. See you on Saturday and we will make you proud. Do take care. Always represent us well."

"I will Uncle," she said in a coyish manner and went off.

Ifeoma had always enjoyed his company and valued his opinion. He was the only one who had asked her how she was faring during her school days and had been generous enough to give her some money a couple of times. He wasn't like her other uncles and aunts who were not that much keen on her welfare.

Her father gave her enough money, but such extra money from Ahubekwe was always a memorable one and made a whole difference to her budget at that given time. On one occasion, she was able to purchase a golden coloured chain wristwatch, which was her first time of having such and she treated it with more preferences when compared to her other brown and black leather watches. Although she no longer wears it, she remembers it vividly and it is now in the possession of *Chinenye -her immediate younger sister,* who admires it so much.

Ideally, Ifeoma was supposed to leave from her parent's house on the wedding day but being that Enugu was quite a distance, they agreed that she joined Ikedinachi in Enugu on Friday so that they would both be in the church at the same time, in order to avoid unnecessary delay and unexpected occurrences. All arrangements were intact, some of Ifeoma and Ikedinachi's cousins in addition to Uchechi, Izuchukwu, and Onyekachi were going to be the flower girls and pageboys. Chinenye would be her maid of honour. So, they went along with her.

# Sixteen

**It** was a 10 a.m. mass, but the bride and groom arrived at the church around 10.30 a.m. despite their efforts to come before the time. They had little chat with the Priest before the celebration. Although most of their guests were yet to arrive, especially their in-laws, the priest told them that he couldn't wait as he was the punctual type and had already said that he had another appointment on that same day.

In fact, if not for the way Ikedinachi and his father had pleaded with him, he would have bluntly told them to choose another Saturday. Luckily for them, Ifeoma's parents arrived almost immediately. So, with both parents and sponsors present there was no need for any further delay.

By the time they knew it, the section of the church where they occupied became filled up. There were several priests. Mr. Ugwu and his in-laws knew many priests and were delighted when some of them made it to their children's wedding despite their busy schedule, inclusive was Fr. Ugoh from their local parish in Achafu.

Fr. Ugoh was the one who gave the sermon and took out time in telling the bride and groom to embrace the future with genuine happiness and love for one another.

"Marriage is an institution initiated by God which man must be committed to. There would be hard times, but with God by your side, you would both pull through."

"Ikedinachi, as you have chosen Ifeoma amongst all the beautiful girls in this world, please do not look at any other girl from today onwards," he joked.

There was an outburst of laughter amongst the audience. They laughed and cheered him.

He then turned to Ifeoma. "Ifeoma, so you have decided to be married to Ikedinachi amongst all the Lagos and Umuezeudo boys? Look at him very well now and make up your mind if you are still in doubt, we can quickly sneak you out through the back door because after blessing both of you today, you are forbidden from talking to another man and have become Ikedinachi's landed property."

It sounded like a joke, but it was a crafty one. Ifeoma giggled where she sat.

"Ikedinachi, am I not right?" the priest asked, and Ikedinachi supported him. He continued and narrated to them the story of a man and his wife. He cleared his throat and began.

"This man and his wife were very fond of each other that they decided to marry one another thinking that all would be well at all times. But as the tides of life began to sweep them in their marital life, they seemed to be two transformed people. The woman who initially calls her husband *"Nkem"* - My Choice - began to refer to him as someone who is 'Useless' -*Onweghi ishi na mmadu*- when she is with friends and relatives, as if literally his brain has been plucked off his head. Whereas, when they initially met and got married, he had a head with a functional brain. At that time, she was very proud of him and acts like she was constantly drunk by their love," he laughed with church members this time.

"From their story, one can tell that they did not groom themselves for contingencies that come with a lifetime commitment. Therefore, since I can see that you both have heads, so please none of you should wake up one morning thinking that the other suddenly has no brain and therefore has become useless."

"Please, I am begging the two of you to always remember today and the promise you are about to make before all the faithful Catholics. We are here with you today, but you will always have to mind your own business. We only want to know that you are faring very well."

"Always learn to communicate effectively and be each other's keeper." Lastly, he told them to make God the head of their home.

He was then joined by the other Priests for the exchange of marital vows while church members clapped for his breath-taking sermon. There were talks and murmurs from the audience.

Many friends of Mr. and Mrs. Ugwu and those from their area came to witness the ceremony.

Luckily, a few seconds before the sermon a Coach from Umuezeudo arrived and the partly filled church turned out to be somewhat crowded.

Ifeoma and Ikedinachi stepped out and were joined by their parents and sponsors.

It was very emotional for Ifeoma's father. He advised and blessed them. This was followed by an encouraging speech from the Ikedinachi's parents as ordered by the officiating priest - *Fr John*.

They happily exchanged their vows and put on their rings. It was at this moment that Ifeoma spotted Cassandra and she could not be happier. She had been worried that she must have forgotten and might not make it.

The whole church celebration went well, and the reception followed almost immediately at the church hall.

Cassandra was able to go across and have a quick girly chat with her friend. They hugged each other like they had not seen in ages. Ifeoma was so pleased to have her best friend around on her wedding day.

"Sandra, I was thinking you were not going to make it," she happily said to her friend.

"Look at you! Why wouldn't I? You look stunning. I never knew you were this beautiful."

"Really?" Ifeoma added. "Thank you, but I prefer the traditional attire to this one."

"Oh! I didn't get to witness that one. Please do not remind me of what I missed."

Ikedinachi and Obinna joined them. It looked more like university days reunion. Some of Ikedinachi's mates in eli mentary school, secondary school, and university were present. Amongst them was Enuma, whom he was delighted to see as he did not know he would bother honouring his invitation.

Cynthia who intentionally wanted to come for the reception was in their midst too. They had a lot of catching up to do, but it did not last long before the attention of bride and groom were needed, and they left.

They chose a corner of the hall and sat together to continue their catch up while admiring their friends.

The reception went smoothly and was really fun, beyond Ikedinachi and Ifeoma's expectations. Ikedinachi's parents did all they could to support their son while Ifeoma's parent's and her uncle Ahubekwe made a huge impact too. In fact, her proud uncle dominated the whole show.

Ahubekwe could not stop decorating their faces with mints of ten-naira notes as though he was spraying mere pieces of papers. Amongst all the numerous gifts their friends and family lavished on them, Ifeoma got a lovely trunk box from Ahubekwe. Their guests ate and drank to their satisfaction, and there were still leftover foods.

However, when sunset began to draw closer, it was time for their in-laws to start heading back home. Ifeoma's siblings went to greet their sister and wished her the best of luck in her new home and took off. Her parents left moments after them as her father do not like late driving for any reason at all.

"Cassandra, hope you will be staying with us?" Ifeoma pleaded.

"Not really Ify, my parents would be expecting me tonight. You know I have not seen them in a while. So, this is a perfect time to spend some time with them."

"Hmmm...."

"I arrived so late last night from Lagos. I guess it is going to be same today. Besides, what do you need me around for? Eh? Am I going to shine torchlight for you tonight?" she teased her.

Ifeoma smiled, and they both laughed.

"Ok, if you insist."

"Yes, I have to. Don't miss me too much; we will see soonest in Lagos."

"Sure! Let me not keep you for so long because Aba is quite a distance. I must get going in order to get a vehicle in the park. Take care of yourself and your husband."

"I will, dear. Thanks for coming. I truly appreciate. My regards to your family. Safe trip."

Cassandra hurriedly left for the park.

By the time they returned home, everyone was exhausted. While Obinna enjoyed his best mate's wedding, he was so much reminded of how he loved and cared for Cynthia.

They acted cool and no one could tell how hard it was for Obinna. Whenever he tried to recall how Cynthia told him that she has chosen a mate in school over him but still cares for him, he got so confused. Could it be that she still loves him and just trying out with a guy that began showing interest in her the moment he left school or something? The latter was obvious.

He told himself it was better he moved on from her. Indeed, times had changed between them, but watching Ikedinachi and Ifeoma filled him with fond memories.

To worsen the whole situation, Cynthia sounded as angelic to him as ever.

# Seventeen

**Hearing** the door being unlocked, Ifeoma ran to get it. It was Ikedinachi, and as he walked in, she hugged him and helped him with the briefcase he was carrying.

"How are you and how was work today?" Ikedinachi asked in a low tone that showed how tired and hungry he was.

"I wanted to surprise you and come home before you today, but you have beaten me," he joked though he meant it.

"Are you serious about that? I had the same thought today. I left earlier so that I can make you your favourite dinner tonight, but I am the lucky one." She gave him that kind of smile that always keeps him on his toes.

"Work was fine Ikem, except for the usual stress. How was yours?"

She helped him unclothe while he changed into a short. Their home was so lovely- ranging from their luxurious and cosy city living room to their old-fashioned bedroom in Enugu.

"My day was not that bad at all, but I was lost in thought over my pretty wife," Ikedinachi said in a tone that depicted he wanted to make someone jealous. He was in madly in love and it was written all over him.

Ifeoma smiled and told him that his food was ready. She sat beside him and admired him as he ate his favourite meal of pounded yam and *egusi* soup. She made *egusi* balls for him too, which he loved so much.

"Ify let's eat. This is wonderful as if you know what my tummy deserves tonight. Please join me," he pleaded.

She insisted she preferred to watch him. She told him that she already ate before his arrival.

Ikedinachi fed her few balls which she ate well and was salivating for more. He told her that it would be nice if she only eats a little before his arrival so that they can both eat together whenever he arrives. She agreed.

Ifeoma was staring at him and could see a lovely and promising future that awaits them. The splendid environment made everything seem so perfect as though they were in a special kind of planet where everything turns out to be rosy all the time.

Within seconds, she heard Ikedinachi's mother calling her and she ran inside to answer her mother-in-law. She woke up and hissed.

She had been dreaming. Why she hissed, she couldn't tell. It was compulsive. She rubbed her eyes and left the bed angrily.

"Are you alright?" Ikedinachi asked her because the hissing was loud and uncalled for.

"Good morning Ikem. Sorry about that. I woke up from a dream."

"What about it? Tell me," Ikedinachi inquired.

"It's not that serious, I am going to tell you but let me greet mama and papa first." She went to greet her mother and father-in-law. She swept the house and was later joined by Adanna as they made breakfast for everyone.

Adanna liked Ifeoma and took her to be the elder sister she never had. Ifeoma did not allow her to do much and made sure she was not late to school. The past few days had been very peaceful for them all. Ifeoma usually gives Adanna extra money for her to buy some snacks for everyone on her way back from school.

Later in the day, they went to the market and purchase some food ingredients to make a lovely dish before Mr. and Mrs. Okoro come back from work.

To some extent, Mrs. Okoro was thinking that her cooking skills would be somewhat jaundiced, but she was damn wrong as Ifeoma cooked very well and everyone in the house liked it and even asked for more. In fact, on the day she made *Owerre* soup, the delicacy was splendid.

When they seem to have the whole house to themselves, she then had time to recall every bit of her dream although she only remembered them in bits, she narrated all of it to him.

Even though Ikedinachi was the kind of person that reads no meaning into dreams, he appeared to have understood the reason for her mood and reaction earlier that morning.

He patted her on the back and told her that her dream was such a beautiful one and teased her to go to sleep again to know if she could come up with a much better version.

"You mean you made me pounded yam and *egusi* soup in the dream? Please make it a reality now."

Ifeoma was trying to read so much meaning into it. She was asking herself a whole lot of questions. Does that mean we are going to be this happy forever?

Is Ikedinachi going to stay with me and forget this trip to the overseas that I don't know what it has in store for us? Besides, in the dream, there were in a lovely stylish apartment that looks so much like one of the beautiful houses that can be seen in Lagos. Why did Ikedinachi's mother have to call her? What did she want to tell her about her son? Why did it end that way? Many questions emerged from the dream, and she lacked adequate answers for them.

At a point, while narrating it to Ikedinachi, she could not tell if it was a dream or a fantasy, but she knew what she was saying.

Unfortunately, Ikedinachi perceived the dream as a lovely and beautiful nothing. There is nothing more he could make out of it Just a dream.

Ifeoma was a bit worried about Ikedinachi's reaction and insisted he should say something meaningful about it.

"I hope you do not take this to be a mere dream?" she asked him.

"What? I don't know why you are taking this seriously."

"Do you feel sick?" He asked her.

Ifeoma shook her head. "I'm fine."

"Wait a minute, don't tell me you need some deliverance. It is just a dream. Ifeoma, since when did you start reading so much meaning into mere dreams? You dreamt last night, and we are going to spend the whole day analysing it."

"I did not mean to upset you. Just that I thought it's not an ordinary one but if you are going to keep sounding this way, let's drop it. I'm fine."

"Better because there are more important things to discuss than this." Ikedinachi yawned and left the room.

He was joined by Ugonna who had already seen him coming to the parlour through the window.

The other day, Mr. Okoro presented the case of his younger brother before him. They wanted him to focus on his study just like they did for him, but he remained so adamant and did not care how they took it. It was quite a difficult situation for his father because he felt they are so much connected and pets him so much. He was told that Ugonna is his grandfather and needed both to be looked after and respected; Mr. Okoro believes in reincarnation.

"Eh... Ugonna, how well do you know this business and how far have you gone? You could at least have completed your school certificate."

Ugonna stretched himself and sat down.

"Brother, I can read and write. I have been making lots of contacts and I'm doing quite well except for money."

"How do you mean money?"

"Money determines the extent you do your business. I am managing the little I have, and I'm yet to hit big. That is what I mean. I don't believe that I have to serve someone for five years to learn trade skills. In one year, I learnt all that I needed to be on my own."

"So, that is why you have decided not to further your studies?" From the way he sounded, Ikedinachi could tell that his kid brother has a mind of his own and didn't want people getting in his way. He admired his guts but did not let him know straight away.

"Yes, brother. I do not think it is compulsory that everyone goes to the university. I guess the essence of schooling is to make a living. I am educated enough and believe I can make more money doing business than doing some sort of office work."

"Well, if you say so. I am not going to sit here and argue with you over completing your education because I have seen you wagging your tongue. Be focused and always listen to papa and mama. Do not give them more headache."

"I would support you later. I am almost bankrupt now. You still remember I am travelling soon?"

"I do. I have friends that have people there. Although they say life there is far better than ours, they still make it clear that most of our brothers over there are suffering and especially, the newly arrived ones. Please do make good contacts to ensure things turn out to be easier for you."

"Yes, they say so, and I know that. But since we are men, we will survive. It is not always that easy."

Ikedinachi felt really surprised by whom his brother has grown to be. He has always seen him as a kid but has managed to have a reasonable conversation with him.

# Eighteen

**Mr.** and Mrs. Okoro's family were finding it difficult to let go of Ikedinachi. Their joy and happiness were short-lived as it was time for Ikedinachi and his wife to leave for Lagos, after which he would then embark on his journey to England soon.

Despite knowing it would happen, they could not still believe how they felt about it as the euphoria that comes with marital bliss almost disappeared.

Mr. Okoro had a hearty and a manly chat with his son and urged him to be prepared for the hard times because they are bound to occur and made him understand that things might not appear that rosy at first like he thinks, but told him that he would be a success just like every other successful person.

As their first son '*okpara,*' he encouraged him to behave himself because much was expected of him by the entire family, especially as he now has a wife to carter for. He gave him his little savings for support.

"Papa, you have already spent enough lately, I can manage. Please keep the money for mama and my siblings."

"We are more worried about you than us."

He was moved by the way his father talked to him. "Thank you, papa." He bowed and collected the money from him.

Mr. Okoro was delighted and relieved that he did so. Despite emptying his pocket, he felt so happy because what he did was to him like paying off a huge debt. He always believed in fending for and supporting his children come what may. At least, Ikedinachi will always remember his little contribution towards his departure to a foreign land.

His entire family prayed for him and promised to keep him in their prayers. Her mother gave him some piece of advice and felt really worried about his welfare and how he was going to cope overseas. Their bond was so much that she wished she could at least be there to ensure she cooks him good meals, if that was the least she could do for him.

Ikedinachi poured out his heart to her and made her understand that he would do all in his power to be the good son they know. He told her that he will always write to them to let them know how he is faring.

A part of his mother wanted him to stay while the other wanted him to go and get a better life. Perhaps, he would come home someday wealthy and rich and transform their standard of living for good. The latter was what kept her going, and she believed God to make it come to pass someday.

She wished him well and reminded him that he needs to do all he could to make sure that Ifeoma joins him soonest to sustain their marriage as they were both young and full of life. Ikedinachi assured her that he has that in his mind.

He received a similar advice in Owerre when they visited Ifeoma's parents. They wished him well and emphasised on how important it is that his wife joins him as quickly as possible. In fact, Ifeoma's mother was of the opinion that he should have planned it, that they travel same time, but her husband convinced her not to worry that it is best that their son-in-law goes first and comes home later for his wife when he ought to have established himself over there.

Mrs. Ugwu somehow understood the situation but was worried about her daughter who will be left behind. She has been concerned about this but Ifeoma talked her off it before the marriage, but now she can't help what she thinks anymore. She would want her child to be pregnant soon so that she would become a grandmother, but she would now have to wait for *until-God-knows-when*.

Many thoughts ran through her mind, those she could verbalise and those she couldn't. In their days, girls were usually not educated and went into marriage early and only did as their parents told them. Times have changed, and many thanks to her husband too. He is an educationist and boasts of good education for all his children both male and female. He is very proud of his daughter and her academic achievements whereas, she thinks tertiary education hinders early marriage amongst girls and has vowed she would make sure her daughters get married while still in school but fears they might not listen to her due to excessive acquisition of knowledge that does make them think they know it all. She knows that she can only try to persuade them.

To make matters worse, in the olden days, girls got married to an elderly man who undoubtedly were capable of their upkeep while Ikedinachi and Ifeoma are more like mates struggling to know their fate in life at 26 and 24 years old respectively. It wasn't as if suitors were not coming for

Ifeoma while she was at university, they were lots of them as she was very gorgeous and ripe for marriage right from her late-teens, but she kept saying she needed to concentrate on her studies. Her father defended her as she was very brilliant, little did they know she was equally studying Ikedinachi in the University at same time.

Nevertheless, Mrs. Ugwu is very much appreciative of her industrious and intelligent daughter, which was an attribute they rarely had in their days. She sighed hoping that all would be well and prayed it all turns out to be worthwhile.

Ifeoma's siblings were excited when they overheard their parents discussing. For all they care, their in-law would be travelling abroad and would soon begin to lavish gift items and money on them. They could not wait for it to happen.

However, they were not alone as Adanna had same thoughts but knew she was going to miss seeing her brother for a while, being that she is fond of him.

Ikedinachi's parents prayed for their son, asking for God's graces and guidance upon him as he journeys into a foreign land.

Earlier, they had a chat with Ifeoma to know if she would prefer to stay with them and work in Enugu than going to stay alone in Lagos, but she said her work environment and conditions in Lagos were satisfactory, which were difficult to come by in her field.

Although Ikedinachi reasoned with his parents, he went for what Ifeoma wanted, and she was right about it. Besides, she has Cassandra who is more like a sister to her, and they work in the same place.

She convinced them that she would manage herself well and promised to come home from time to time. If it is something that she can easily forfeit, she would have considered that but she felt deep inside her that it was not going to be a good decision had she given in. It was as though she had turned their first request down, but it appeared her hands were tied up and she did hope they understood and respected her wish.

Her father-in-law made her understand that he only wanted her to be safe and feel at home but could understand her plight while her mother-in-law was not so pleased that she preferred staying on her own in Lagos.

At that moment, the fact that Ikedinachi would be leaving her in the next couple of days made her head spin, and she couldn't handle any further erratic occurrences. She appeared calmed but was very worried as they still had few days to themselves.

It was sunset, and they all slept peacefully after a day filled with talks, preparations, and emotions. Early in the morning the next day, they all escorted them off to the motor park where they got on a bus that headed to Lagos. The way they all came with them and hugged each other passionately clearly told onlookers that it was not a common farewell.

Ikedinachi's father told him to always remember all that he had told him and remain focused. Her mother cried and was still able to mumble some blessings upon him.

"My son, may the God-of-all-travellers see you through. May he be your father, mother, and siblings in that foreign soil. As she talked, she cried, and her husband dragged her off to avoid creating scenes. Other travellers were already staring at them. Ikedinachi hugged his siblings. Adanna told him she was going to miss him while he reassured her and told her to always be a good girl that she is.

"Take care of the family in my absence," he said to Ugonna.

"I will," Ugonna nodded and shook hands with him in acceptance and wished him well.

It was an emotional moment for them all.

When the bus was filled with passengers, they started hitting the roads that lead to Lagos. Ikedinachi placed his left hand on his wife's neck, and she leaned towards him. They were both lost in thoughts and did not talk much throughout the journey.

# Nineteen

**They** got to Lagos at about 6 p.m. and were very tired. Ifeoma was able to tidy the house a bit to at least make it habitable for them to lay their heads for the night. They ate the snacks they purchased on the road and retired for the day.

They woke up feeling very exhausted as though their energy was sapped from the journey.

"What a trip! I am glad how things have unfolded," Ikedinachi uttered.

"Hmmm, we have done a lot within the past few weeks," she replied.

"And there are still few more important ones left." She was not sure if the right word was 'more important' or 'major.'

Meanwhile, a lot has happened lately, but she could not still bring herself to terms with the fact that Ikedinachi would be leaving her soon. At first, she kind of liked the idea, but presently, she couldn't tell why she seemed so cold about everything whereas, they have both planned things and hoped they all fall neatly into place without much difficulties. Now it's all happening.

They had a breakfast of tea and bread.

"I will be leaving for the office soon. What about you? You don't behave like you are going to work today. What's your plan?" he stroked her face.

"I will be going to my place later and will go to market on my way back. Will report to work tomorrow."

"Ok, is there anything you want me to help you with in your house? You know we are now living here, no more weekends or visits." They both laughed.

"I need not be told. Besides, I want to spend every nick of time with you. But since my rent is not yet due, I might leave some stuffs there and move them gradually. I'm here," she said in a reassuring manner.

"If you say so." Ikedinachi dressed up and left for work.

"Ehmm... you mentioned going to the market. Would this be enough?" he offered her some squeezed currencies he shoved out from his pocket.

"Ikem don't worry I will manage the one I have. I have some money with me."

"I know... add it to the one you have. I am lucky to have a supportive wife, you know; who doesn't want her husband to be spending all the time, but I want you to always have extra."

He squeezed the money into her hand and hugged her.

"See you in the evening."

"Bye Ikem." She was all smiles.

She went to bed for a nap. Good thoughts filled her mind. She so much wanted the next few days to be memorable for both of them. Their happiness and joy were all that mattered to her.

Later, she did some mopping and properly cleaned the entire flat. She unpacked their suitcases, bags, and the foodstuffs that her parents and Ikedinachi's parents gave them. It equally enabled her to know what they had and what she needed to buy in the market.

She decided to make a lovely *Nsala* soup for her husband since they came back with some *bonga* fish. She intends to buy other remaining condiments in the market alongside some household items. She tried to be time conscious as she wanted the food to be ready before her husband comes home. *The dutiful wife just arrived.*

At work, Ikedinachi had lots of pleading and explanation to do. Most of his colleagues were thrilled to hear of his marriage and congratulated him. He went over to his boss and thanked him for his assistance and how he had been very considerate with him.

However, some of his mates were not so pleased with him especially since he neither mentioned his trip to the east nor his wedding to them. Some took it very personal and overreacted whereas it was pretty obvious that they would not have made it to his wedding, but since he was already sentenced and guilty of the crime in question, he could do nothing less than to explain himself to them the much he could and hoped they understand and pardon him.

However, there were a few who were sensible enough to talk to him in a more reasonable manner despite how they viewed his decision.

He later got himself programmed to pleading with them and knew it was going to be like that for a while.

"I guess that is the price you pay for being the social and the chatty type," he told himself.

He asked after his colleague Frank, the one who was organising his travelling documents and was told that he was last seen over a week ago. He did not let that worry him as he already knew his residence in Satellite town.

He could not wait for closing time go to go home to his beloved wife. The mere thought of that gladdened his heart. Besides, it was their honeymoon period as well.

It was equally a hectic day for Ifeoma. When she got to her yard, her neighbours interrogated her about her absence which she handled quite well. With the ring on her finger, she had better start saying something they simply wanted to hear. She told them that she did not want to blow things out as it was sort of rushed and she could not get to let the cat out of the bag like that. She tried to conceal some information she considered vital and private from them. Well, they congratulated her and seemed not to probe further.

"Iyawo, your kids are growing fast," she added as the kids played beside each other.

*"Yes oh. Na God oh! Wetin I know sey I dey do sef. Hardship plenty,"* she hissed.

*"Abeg no talk that one. You and your oga dey try for them well."* Ifeoma offered them the biscuits she bought for them.

"Have you said thank you Auntie!" she shouted to them.

"Thank you, Auntie," they mumbled in their soft voices and ran off.

*"You sef! You just dey like do your own thing your own way. Hope say na that your Oga wey I sabi? Abi another one come chance am?"* Iyawo asked.

Ifeoma laughed at the question and the way she eyed her as she asked her.

*"Tell me... I wan know o,"* Iyawo insisted.

*"Na him.* He is my one and only," Ifeoma replied in a very feminine and proud tone.

"Ah!" Iyawo sh outed in ecstasy placing her hand over her mouth.

"I dey very happy for the two of una. If you know as my heart dey take do me now, I don dey like your person and how you dey run your things teetee."

*"Commot there!" she shouted to one of his little boys who was playing with a bucket of dirty water left by other residents. "This boy no go gree me talk better thing,"* she hurriedly went and dragged him out.

*"How Paul and him wife them? Thelma and the rest?"* Ifeoma was asking about the other neighbours.

*"They all fine... for the ones wey I take my two eyes see."*

*"Iyawo I go leave you.* I have many things lined up for the day. I go enter market."

*"Which day you go visit us again?"*

*"I go dey come dey go for now sha but the thing be say I no live here again,"* Ifeoma smiled.

*"Help me greet others when they come back from work."*

*"I know that kind thing jare. Na so I dey bi. Who talk say better thing no sweet? Your own better o,"* She added and went inside her room to know what her active kids were up to.

*"Buy better thing go cook orishirishi for your oga o,"* Iyawo shouted from her room.

*"Hahaha... ok o."*

Ifeoma checked the time and seemed to be some minutes behind like she had speculated. Luckily for her, Mama Funmi a very close friend of hers who she knew that would have wanted to know what actually happened in detail travelled to her hometown for a burial according to Iyawo. She was the only one whom she briefed about her trip, and she gave her some piece of advice and asked for

God's blessings upon her. In a strange place like Lagos miles away from home, she was so fortunate to have a woman like that as a neighbour.

By the time she got home, she was very tired and sweating. She first had a cold bath and headed for the kitchen. Feeling refreshed and clothed in a sleeveless top and wrapper, she set out for what she knew how to do best and was in her best frame of mind. She was in a hurry as she wanted to prepare a lovely dish before her husband returns from work. Within minutes, her pots were boiling and oozing out the kind of aroma that would make even someone who is not hungry salivate unknowingly.

Soup was ready, and she steamed some meat she bought as well for stew she intended to make the next day.

Coincidentally, at almost the same time she had finished pounding yam, Ikedinachi came back from work. Looking very tired and with his nostrils filled with the aroma of the delicacy his wife is preparing, he fell onto the sofa.

Ifeoma quickly washed her hands, adjusted her wrapper and went over to welcome him.

"Good evening Ikem, you look so tired."

"Tired and famished. I am already salivating for your dish."

Ifeoma went off to the kitchen. Within seconds, she appeared with a tray containing their well-prepared dinner. As they ate, she looked admiringly at her husband.

Having eaten halfway and probably satisfied his hunger to a reasonable extent, Ikedinachi licked his fingers one after another.

"Ify, this is one of the best foods I have had in a very long time. In fact, you are the best cook so far, after my mother," he said the last bit in a very funny and little tone.

"I know. I agree... everyone's mother is the best cook." They sent more balls of pounded yam with chunks of fish and meat down their throat as they chatted.

Her heart was filled with joy because she likes to know that her man loves and enjoys every bit of her cooking. At least, it was worth the effort. That alone gives her great joy.

She felt very confident and proud of herself. In her culture, a woman is expected to be a quintessential domesticated person.

"Work was pretty okay, though tiring, but you needed to see how I had to explain myself to all my colleagues. They were all on my neck trying to know why I chose to go about my trip and our wedding without their knowledge. At one point, I didn't find it funny."

"Ah Ah! It must have been some kind of interrogating sessions for you," she joked.

"At a time, I just felt like they should just let me be, even those that you know that they simply do not care much about you, let alone attending the occasion were all talking," he said.

"Can you imagine?"

"Yes, I know that kind of attitude. Hehehe! I'm going to have my own encounter tomorrow, but I do not think it would be that probing like yours."

While kneeling beside the bed, Ifeoma in a very soft tone led in the night prayer. Cuddling each other, their eyes gradually closed.

# Twenty

"**Hey!** Look at you. Where have you been hiding? You just disappeared," a colleague asked Ifeoma.

Ifeoma ran her eyes all over her body – *in response "look at you"* and her face glittered with smile.

"Good morning, I was off work for a while but fully back now."

"Oh! Congrats on your marriage!" Her eyes gazed at her wedding ring.

"You look so refreshed dear."

"Thank you."

Some of her colleagues knew about her marriage when Cassandra decided to make it public following her attendance at the occasion although Ifeoma had told her not to spread the news just yet. She chatted with others too and headed off to her section.

Cassandra was pleased to see her back and updated her with all that happened while she was away. It was then that she disclosed to her how Muyiwa reacted when he heard about her wedding.

"Oh! Was it that bad for him?" Ifeoma asked like she didn't know he had a crush on her. Not that she doesn't know, but she just didn't know he couldn't hide it from others.

"What?" she screamed. "Leave that one *joor*. I call them distractors, or you don't mind?"

Cassandra laughed in her usual tone while Ifeoma smiled and shook her head.

Closing her ears with both hands, "Cassandra! No way. You!" in that tone she usually calls her when she senses she was being mischievous. But she still loves her to bits.

As Ifeoma went back to her desk, she met an angry old woman who was amongst other numerous customers waiting to be served. On her arrival, the single line split drawing some people to her section.

Tending to angry customers was not strange for Ifeoma, but she could tell from the woman's unusual behaviour that she was going to be trouble.

Note currencies are meant to be sorted out and arranged before going to the service points, but the woman still had some squeezed notes with her and dumped them on Ifeoma's counter.

"Please sort out the rest; I have been here for so long. I don't know what you people are being paid for by the way. For nearly one hour only one person was left to serve everyone here," the woman hissed.

Her plea was actually of no use because she sounded very harsh and she knew it. Perhaps, she didn't know when she said please. As she talked, others joined her like they had been waiting for someone to start the complaints.

Ifeoma knows how to be calm even when customers shout at the top of their voices. She tried handling this one in the same manner.

"Ma, you are supposed to count all these notes and assemble them for me," she told her and at the same time picked them up one after the other to arrange them. Obviously, the woman was a trouble-maker, so those behind her simply didn't grumble over that. Besides, she came before them and is an elderly. Case settled.

"Why are they this rumpled?" Ifeoma asked in a very nice tone as though she was trying to engage her in a meaningful conversation.

"Is it not government money? Or is it *kantafiti*? How many times do you people give someone *chassis* and we don't bring them back to you? When you send out rumpled money, they come back to you rumpled."

"Anyway, it is from a collection by my fellow town women." She adjusted her loosened abada.

"Ok ma, now I know. Please ma, next time someone should count them well before you bring them. Why are they even sending you?"

"They didn't send me," she cut her in. "I offered to come, and we already know the amount."

Ifeoma sorted out the money and the figures corresponded, but she urged her to make sure it is always correct before coming to the bank.

"After all this time spent here, am eventually leaving," she hissed. "You people think we leave our houses to come and do your work and sleep here with you."

As she left, Ifeoma sighed and focused on other customers who watched the whole drama.

"Ify, that woman was very annoying. You know your friend Cassandra wouldn't have taken that from her. She would have at least sat down by the corner, count all her money and then come back to her," her colleague teased her. "But that's true you know."

"I pitied the old woman jare. You can't just please her. On a good day, they would meet Sandra, and she would give them a befitting treatment though she treats them well sometimes." They both laughed.

---

Ikedinachi was finally able to meet up with Frank after over two weeks of trying to reach him without any luck. He was relieved at last. As for Ifeoma, a part of her didn't want anything to separate them, not just yet.

Frank reappeared at work on a Tuesday and headed straight for Ikedinachi after meeting with their boss.

"Guy how far?" He shook hands with Ikedinachi who was surprised to see him.

"I'm good. Where have you been?"

"Marriage sure looks good on you," Frank teased him.

"What do you see? Thanks though."

"Were you told I checked on you?" Ikedinachi asked as he wasn't sure the man he met on the day he went over to his place would have bothered to deliver his message.

"Eh... I arrived very late last night, but I can remember Emma trying to tell me someone from work came, but I didn't pay much attention to that. There wasn't need for that."

"*How far? Hope your remaining balance dey down?* Things don almost ready; your travel documents should be available soon. In fact, some are with me," Frank updated him.

"Are you serious?" was all Ikedinachi was able to spit out after moments of panicking.

He scratched his head. "So, when will all of it be ready?"

"*No worry. Me and them still dey talk. We go finalise everything by Friday.*"

"But wait, how come no one knew your whereabouts?"

*"Leave that thing. Do they tell me before they commot? Everybody dey mind em business here. I only told my Oga. I know say you go dey worry, but I know say I go come back soon sha."*

"Look here," he handed over to him some documents and briefed him on how far they have actually gone. It was not till then that Ikedinachi finally believed that once more his colleague was doing his best for him.

The day was already going well for Ikedinachi and at same time reality was beginning to set in. From what his friend told him, he would be leaving almost soon because they will as well purchase his ticket as part of the package.

They discussed the financial aspect and how much he was going to give him. Though he didn't expect that he was going to spend a large sum of money on this, he was somewhat pleased with the cost so far. At least, Frank was being honest.

The doorknob was turned leaving the door a bit open.

"Frank? Is that you? I heard a voice that sounded like yours. *Na your eyes be this?*" Stella, one of their colleagues uttered and left almost immediately.

"Wait abeg!" Frank shouted.

As they were almost done, he rushed his last words and went after Stella.

Ikedinachi went for few minutes break to get some fresh air in order to allow the latest news sink in. He was filled with ecstasy that the room didn't seem to contain him.

Some minutes later, he went back to his desk and worked in a happier and undisturbed state of mind. For the first time in a very long time, his mind was at rest about the travelling issue.

139

# Twenty-One

Weeks passed by and only few days to the day Ikedinachi would be leaving for England. All the while, he has been very apprehensive of the fact that he would travel but never gave in to the other part of him that preferred to be sober and ponder about leaving Ifeoma behind and how he would cope. Instead, he chose to be strong.

In fact, over the past few days, Ifeoma had been unnecessarily ill. If she was not having a terrible headache, it would be fever or extreme fatigue, by the time you knew it, she already whimpered.

Ikedinachi felt he just needed to be strong for the two of them and had to man-up. He felt so helpless each time Ifeoma cried. Lately, it was either he bumped into her crying in a corner of the room or she came out with swollen eyes.

Ifeoma became so emotional, which troubled Ikedinachi. But knowing that she was in no way the likes of 'Ahuruole' in *The Concubine* novel, he knew she would soon be fine. He was so much hopeful of that.

He knew it was a momentary issue and hoped she takes good care of herself in his absence. Ikedinachi was lost in deep thought about his emotional wife.

He had sent a letter to his parents letting them know that he was leaving soon. He tactically prepared himself in his own little way for the journey and the life overseas that awaits him. To say that it doesn't trouble him; what would become of him in overseas, how he would cope in a foreign land and that revolves around it- would be a fat lie.

Nevertheless, going abroad to better his life had always been his dream and he was going to seize this precious opportunity with the very hope and trust in God that it turns out well as he expected. This forms the huge part of all his daily prayers.

Ifeoma spent majority of the night packing her husband's suitcase. She had taken time to dry some vegetables like bitter leaf for him and bought some local food condiments too. It was as though she was trying to make sure he does not starve in his first days over there. Ifeoma packed lots of clothes in addition to the ones Ikedinachi already chose. She was able to sneak in some that she knew he might find useful.

On the morning of Ikedinachi's departure, it was as if someone had died and everyone happened to be in a mourning mood. He woke up having a mixed feeling.

At the airport, Ifeoma stayed with him till check-in time. They both felt so helpless as Ifeoma's tears went out of control, but he had to go. He hugged her, squeezed and kissed her. It was difficult to let go of each other, but their time was up.

"Take good care of yourself for me," he uttered.

She nodded and managed to say, "I will."

"Be good Ikem; I will miss you so much."

She sobbed and stepped aside while Ikedinachi dragged his hand luggage towards the boarding gate but turned back and waved her bye for the last time. She waved back with her right hand letting the other one run freely between her mouth and her hair in a very confused and shattered manner. She watched him till his image disappeared.

It was then that she became aware of people who had been staring and those stealing glances at her, she pulled herself together and cleaned her eyes while some teardrops rolled down her cheeks. A lady walked up to her in concern.

"Hi, is he travelling abroad the first time?" she asked in a sympathetic tone.

"Yes..." Ifeoma tried to put on a smile while she blew her nose with a hankie. "Sorry about that."

"Yes... his first time."

"I can imagine how you feel. It's alright. It is perfectly normal for you to feel the way you do right now. Do try to be strong and hope he does same too. I remember my first experience, but now we handle it better," the lady told her.

She looked towards the direction of her family; a man who was playing with a little boy.

"You have a lovely family," Ifeoma complimented.

"I thank God my dear. I will leave you now. I'm Angela by name and yours?"

"Ifeoma. Thanks for your concern, I feel much better now." The chat brightened her face a bit and she left the airport.

Elsewhere on the plane, Ikedinachi was lost in thought and tears clouded his eyes. In a tactful manner, he cleaned them as they were about to drop to avoid the passenger beside him knowing what he was battling with.

Moments later, he was able to get his head around it and became a cheerful travel companion.

# Twenty-Two

Initially, Ikedinachi found England extremely challenging but believed he did not need to call home for help. Settling into an absolute different culture got the best part of him. He was determined that it was only a matter of time for him to cope well, despite the culture shock.

John welcomed Ikedinachi and made him comfortable. He allowed a couple of days to pass by before keeping Ikedinachi abreast of what is obtainable and what is not in the UK for him. As it were early days for him in the country, John knew what it felt like to be new in a strange country and was willing to help. He intended to ensure that Ikedinachi felt at home in his one-bedroom apartment. However, he would like him to leave his apartment the moment he gets a job and can afford to pay his bills.

Amongst numerous difficulties, job hunting was one of the most difficult challenges Ikedinachi encountered. Getting a job and as quickly as possible meant a whole lot to him, to enable him to pay bills, at least. It was during this frustrating job searching period that he realised that things were not as easy as they really appeared to be. He remembered the saying, "All that glitters are not gold' and taught it perfectly defines his current situation. Initially, he was picky about jobs options including cleaning and hospitality works. These are jobs he would have never laid hands on if it were to be in his home country - *Nigeria*.

That made him wonder if he had left home to become a white man's slave? For how long? Nothing was that easy for him, all his encounters had followed rigorous processes, and he did not find that encouraging, but he never relented. He recalled that his father once told him not to be ashamed of whatsoever that will enable him to survive in life and be optimistic at all times. He felt consoled.

When he noticed that such odd jobs were the norm in London coupled with lots of accumulating bills, he had to grab one. Besides, it would enable him to eat and take care of the fast bills. The first job he got was a cleaning job, where he had to go to sweep and tidy different offices in the morning. As if the menial job on its own is not enough, he had to comport himself well and show that he was capable of delivering effectively, he had to prove that he was really interested in the job. He would wake up early and tried as fast as he could to clean different offices, which meant more money.

Before he knew it, a colleague told him about a restaurant job where he has to work in the kitchen. His duties were mainly to wash plates and everything that needed to be washed. At this point in his life, he was so engulfed in work life that all that counted was how much he made from his two jobs. He guarded them with all seriousness because he knew they were not that easy to come by. The aspect of him that would normally worry about the sort of job he should not stoop low to do was long buried. He went from one job to another and eventually got a stable one.

He wrote letters to his family back home in Nigeria to let them know that he was doing his best to make ends meet and also to know how everyone was doing.

The first letter he got from Ifeoma was to inform him about her pregnancy. Ifeoma found out that she was pregnant weeks after he travelled but waited to hear from him before informing him. Her parents and Ikedinachi's parents were extremely happy when she broke the news to them. Mrs. Okoro asked her to come and stay with her in the east, but she declined her request. She told her that she can come and stay with them whenever she decides. Her mother promised to be with her during the arrival of the baby. They could not wait to have their first grandchild.

Ifeoma was overjoyed when Ikedinachi wrote to let her know he was fine in England and that England was what he had imagined it to be: a beautiful nation where everyone seemed to be so serious at all times and minded their businesses.

Ikedinachi could not believe that he was going to be a father. He felt like that was all the boost he needed to remain focused it in London. He now has dependents.

John's cousin- Seye- had rung him from University to inform him that he was having accommodation issues and wanted to stay with him. He tried to explain to him that he had someone with him and it was not a good time for him, but the situation got worse when Seye confided in him and told him that his Spanish girlfriend was pregnant. They argued over it at length, but he finally asked him to move in with him after several questions and scoldings. He was family, and he couldn't turn his back on him which meant Ikedinachi would be getting the boot.

Ikedinachi got home and carefully unpacked the groceries he had bought when John walked in from the room.

"Guy, what's up?"

"Good. I didn't know you were in. You are not watching the match?" Ikedinachi asked and quickly turned the television on.

"Oh! I completely forgot its today." He joined him. They enjoyed some drinks while they watched the match. Liverpool FC was playing Everton in a heated Merseyside derby as they call it and John deliberated on how to break the news to Ikedinachi. He had wanted to give him reasonable time to settle, but with Seye's issue, he had no other option.

At the end, he told Ikedinachi that there was something important he wanted to discuss with him. Ikedinachi became anxious as that was unusual.

"Is everything ok?" Ikedinachi asked.

"The thing is…" he sat up.

"Are we cool?" Ikedinachi asked still wondering what it could be John wants to discuss with him.

John explained the whole situation to him and how desperate his cousin was. In the end, Ikedinachi asked him to give him at least a week to see what he can arrange for himself. Ikedinachi was like a mate as they had no issues throughout his stay with him, and he was the best housemate he had ever lived with. John was truly sorry for the inconvenience although he knew it was bound to happen at some point though.

In the same way, Ikedinachi least expected the news he got as he has only spent a year in England. Luckily, he had been able to save some money from the jobs he had been doing. John offered to help him to find a place, and after a week, he moved out. He thanked him for looking after him, and told him he would stay in touch.

He secured a room in a shared apartment in Tottenham, north London. The room was carefully furnished and he made sure it had all the essential things he needed in it. It was overtly lovely and cosy and remained his safe haven. Comfort is something Ikedinachi cannot compromise regardless of his situation. It was as though he was beginning to find his ground in the Whiteman's land. He became fully independent and gradually was able to manage himself.

He thought about Ifeoma and their son. He knew that there were so many things that he needed to put right. Though he struggled, he knew that his family coming to join him would be a fantastic idea, and he pondered over it. *If only it would be that easy?* He wondered when it would be and shook his head in disbelief.

From time to time, he tried to get himself acquainted with this strange country and its austere culture. He attended local meetings in his neighbourhood to enable him socialise and develop relationships. He studied maps to discover new places to tour and checked notice boards for upcoming events he could attend in his spare times.

The fact that he came from a strict Catholic family background made it difficult for him to worship in nearby Anglican and Pentecostal churches which were predominant in the area he lived. Eventually, he located St. Mellitus in Finsbury grove which was quite a distance and would go there every Sunday morning. He found the mass celebration very interesting and compassionate and was pleased with the way people make out time for church, despite their bizarre lifestyle he had noticed. In his culture, most people are very religious but what he sees around him were those whose were more scientific than religious.

St. Mellitus is among the few churches in London that integrate certain African cultures into its mass celebration. They celebrate masses in various languages and of which *Igbo* is included. *Igbo* mass celebrations usually holds every third Sunday of each month and often lures many Nigerians especially the Igbos and their acquaintances to the church. Their choir performance was always lovely and appealed to the souls of numerous worshippers.

Most fascinating for Ikedinachi was when he discovered that mass celebration was available in his own mother tongue - *Igbo*.

To put icing on the cake, he had a wonderful and unique experience the first time he attended reconciliation service as he simply sat beside the Priest and poured out his troubled heart [confessed his sins] in a friendly and chatty manner though fundamental absolution and penance accompanied it. This made him talked more freely and at length when compared with the former way of kneeling on the confessional and in most cases not seeing the face of the Priest back home, where it strictly follows a certain pattern. He became pleased with his spiritual life in his new environment.

---

In Ikedinachi's bid to lead a better life, he thought of securing admission into a university. He successfully gained admission into City University London to study Business Studies. Moreover, it would enable him to apply for visa extension when the time comes.

Ikedinachi worked earnestly to combine work and studies irrespective of the high cost of living in England. At first, it seemed he was driving himself to breaking point, but he kept going as he knew it was for a while. There were days he barely had five hours to rest, eat, sleep, and prepare for either work or school.

His wife and son were his inner drive whenever he felt weak. He lives and works for them. Ifeoma frequently wrote, especially to tell him how his little one was doing. He was named after him- Ikedinachi Jr. Ikedinachi writes her whenever he could and managed to send them his love and gifts. He was pleased with the way Ifeoma sent him photos of Junior.

Ikedinachi was able to adjust to the school system and tried as much as he could not to miss lectures, despite arriving late most times to lecture room. School meant so much to him because he knew he had to make better grades. In no little time, he found out that there are people struggling like him. He was able to make new friends but bonded more easily with fellow Africans, especially those from his country.

Dayo was one of his friends and a Nigerian too. He had been living in the UK for more than six years and seemed to know more about the country, at least, when compared to Ikedinachi. He studied his first degree in the same university, knew his way around the campus, and therefore, was willing to assist Ikedinachi where necessary despite their clashes of personality. Eventually, they became close friends.

# Twenty-Three

Cassandra made sure she supported her friend as she knew how difficult working and looking after a baby could be. She regularly visited her, and they have grown so close that most of their friends see them as sisters.

Mrs. Ugwu stayed with Ifeoma for three months and went back to the east as she needed to cater for her husband and Ifeoma's younger siblings. Since her departure, it has not been that easy for Ifeoma.

Ikedinachi's mother came later and had stayed for a month and asked her to bring the baby home when she could for her husband to see.

By the time Ifeoma returned to work, there had been some new staff, and Muyiwa now works next to him. She knew how he feels about her and was not comfortable having him that close. Most times, she tried to be formal with him, but Muyiwa would always find a way to bring up a topic that was not work-related.

Each morning, Muyiwa would admire her from hair to toes. It was as though she appeared to be prettier than she was before her pregnancy. He liked the way she styles her long curly brown afro hair. Regardless of what she wears, her shoulders were always raised as though the best seamstress had made the best available shoulder pads specially for her-all in Muyiwa's eyes.

On countless times, Ifeoma had noticed the way he looked at him. Unknown to her, he had been stalking her and knew where she lived.

"Ify baby, I had this dream about us."

"Dream? You and who makes up the 'us'?" Ifeoma was in the course of trying to get used to his annoying conversations, but she had begun to find him very irritating.

"It was a beautiful one, you were smiling, and I wondered why you don't smile like that when you are in the office. Please, can you loosen that frowned face?" Ifeoma was boiling inside but did not say a word.

"I was in your place, and you made this soup for me, and we eat together. I fed you-"

"Stop it! What is wrong with you? I am a married woman. Leave me alone!" Ifeoma shouted.

"Please Ify, lower your voice; you don't want people to hear us. The thing is, I like you a lot, don't tell me you don't know. I will not do anything that will change you from a married woman to an unmarried one. You and your husband on the one lane, me and you on another lane."

"Muyiwa, I can see you have gone crazy completely," Ifeoma hissed and brought out piles of receipts that needed to be sought out. She did not pay further attention to him.

"Just give me a chance. You will benefit too. Anyway, I'm here for you anytime."

At lunch break, Ifeoma did not look her usual self which made Cassandra wondered what the problem was.

"Are you ok Ify? Is anything the matter?"

"I'm fine," Ifeoma replied and hissed.

Cassandra moved closer to her. "Fine and hissing don't go together, so talk to me."

"Isn't that Muyiwa guy that has been disturbing me since the first day I got back from maternity leave. He talks all time, telling me stupid things I do not want to hear. Any more of it, I will report him," she sounded a bit relieved.

"Haba! I didn't know things has gone this bad between you two?"

"What do you mean by 'you two'?"

"I don't know whose idea it was that he works next to me."

"I know. I knew that you wouldn't like it at all, but you know how it is now – we don't have powers when the bosses implement their change."

"This change was uncalled for. What happened to his office?"

"But you two are adults and should be able to iron things out. He can't be making you feel this upset."

"I have tried to talk to him, but he does not get it. It is as if talking to him worsens the whole situation." She was right, to Muyiwa, her attention and voice fill him up; whether she talked or screamed, he would skip lunch breaks just to be next to her.

"I can tell him off you know," Cassandra suggested.

"I hope he gets the message."

"Cheer up please. Have you heard from your husband lately?"

"Yes," Ifeoma's face glittered.

"See the look on your face now! Maybe, if he had been around, you wouldn't be getting upset over little things."

"Cassandra! If not that I've known you for years, I would have said you and Muyiwa are on a mission to drive crazy in this place, but it won't work."

"How do you mean?"

"Ikedi has been making plans for me and junior to join him. He had started the process; I am expecting his letter soonest."

"Ah!!!" Cassandra screamed, "you had better news and you did not tell me."

They both hugged each other.

"This is good. How is Junior?" Cassandra asked.

"He is doing good dear. Getting bigger every single day."

"Tell him aunty Cassandra will come during the weekend."

They both went back to work.

# Twenty-Four

Ikedinachi made the necessary preparation for Ifeoma and their son to join him in the UK. He made good contacts and gathered all the required documents. He had taken months to inquire on what documents were needed. Dayo had told him to simply get a solicitor to do the job for him. Dayo's parents are very rich and would normally get someone paid to assist them with any application regardless of the contents of the form. Most times, Dayo only gets to know the contents of the application when it requires an interview.

He tried to convince Ikedinachi to get a solicitor as he knew how his friend could not wait to be joined by his family. Ikedinachi was reluctant to heed to his advice; it was not that Dayo was wrong, but he had gone through the form and had been able to provide what was required. Besides, meeting immigration experts are not free. Maybe Dayo did not know that not everyone can afford such services.

Dayo was surprised when Ikedinachi informed him about the success of his application for his family.

"Well done my man. You deserved it," Dayo said.

"Thanks for your support."

"We gonna celebrate. Your hard work paid off." Dayo was happy for him.

On their way out, they ran into an old man who waved at Ikedinachi, and he waved back.

"Why is the white old man waving at you?" Dayo asked.

"We live in same block, but for some reasons when I moved in newly, he would not respond when I greet him. I see him often, maybe he is a pensioner - that is if he had ever worked. On one occasion, he struggled with opening the door, and his shopping bags were all over the place. I went over and helped him with the door and his bags, and that was the first time I heard him speak.

"Thank you," was all he said.

"Hey! See my Naija good boy. Who sent you? I would not bother saying hello to such people let alone the second and subsequent times."

"I think he doesn't talk often."

"He could be a ghost," Dayo joked.

"There is something queer about him. Since then he only waves when he sees me, and I do same."

They went to a restaurant and had a good time. Ikedinachi wrote to Ifeoma and updated her about the success of the application.

---

In Lagos, Ifeoma woke up feeling as though for some reasons a lovely spell was casted on her day. Having done her morning routine of praying, tidying up, getting Junior ready and dropped him off at nursery, she left for work.

It's been five years since that cold and miserable night Ikedinachi waved goodbye to her at the airport. It has turned out to be a huge learning curve for her, from the lonely nights to the tedious unending months of pregnancy to the challenges of joggling work with raising Ikedinachi junior, let alone, the unending flirtations by Muyiwa. She felt like throwing a party when he was transferred to their Ibadan branch about eight months ago. She is certain that Cassandra had a hand in that though she has never owned up to it. She couldn't believe just how things have worked out like clockwork. She felt like congratulating herself for a job well done, so far.

She received a letter, and as usual, it was from her Ikedinachi. Her heart swelled with joy as she opened and read the letter.

Three weeks ago, Ikedinachi wrote to inform her about the travel arrangements.

Ifeoma screamed so loud almost forgetting that she was in the office. This time, Ikedinachi had given her the biggest surprise of her life by telling her that he will be coming to get her and their son in few weeks' time.

She was so overjoyed. She could not contain the joy alone that comes with going to join Ikedinachi; now she has to deal with seeing Ikedinachi come home in few weeks' time.

To her, that could be in two weeks' time or so. Maybe less.

It was as though Ifeoma's head was going to burst with happiness and excitement. She had lots of ideas going through her head. So many fantasies, so very many.

Ifeoma's day and even week was already enlightened by the letter from her husband.

Unknown to Ikedinachi's family, he has decided to visit home and at the same time take his beloved wife and son to England. The *"always waving old man"* turned out to be the father of Sir Henry Walters, the CEO of Walters, one the foremost accounting firms in Leeds. A little recommendation from Sir Walters landed Ikedinachi a dream job in such a prestigious firm.

Ikedinachi arrived in Lagos in less than two weeks and went straight to their home. It was on a Saturday morning and Ifeoma was in bed playing with Junior, as their weekends simply meant no school and no office work.

Ikedinachi had arrived with airport taxi. He walked into their apartment with his suitcases. Ifeoma could not believe her eyes when she saw her charming Ikedinachi standing right before her.

At first, it felt like she was seeing a ghost, but it was a real person.

"Ifym…."

"Ikem…."

They both rushed for each other and hugged dearly. Ikedinachi was plastering kisses all over her face. Junior who was ardently observing them all this while and could not help but observe that the man with her mummy bears a striking resemblance to the image which adorn their sitting room and bedroom. They untangled and Ikedinachi reached for Junior, who had a striking resemblance to him, but he took a step back.

It was the first time he set his eyes on his little boy although Ifeoma had been trying to update him about their son's progress by sending him photos and milestone news. At a time, Ifeoma even measured his small his foot length with broomstick and sent to Ikedinachi to enable him get pairs of shoes for their child.

Ikedinachi stared at his son and all he could see was a *mini* him. His hands were still stretched when junior after a little scrutiny looked at his mother and curiously asked, "Mummy is this my daddy?"

"Yes son, he is your father". Ifeoma answered like she had waited her entire life for Jr to ask that question.

Little Junior did not require further persuasion as he rushed into the waiting arms of his father who grabbed him, threw him up severally while tickling him at the same time. They were all laughing and giggling that Ikedinachi did not know when he slipped and sent everyone crashing to the bed, which if nothing else intensified the laughter. After laughing for what seemed an eternity, everyone was exhausted.

The serene quietness was broken when junior looked straight into her father moist eyes and said, "Daddy! do it again".

"God is great is His work and His timing", Ikedinachi thought out loud. It was not the same as the pictures he had seen over time; it felt like he was getting to know about his son for the very first time. He carried him up, dropped him, carried him again, hugged and kissed him.

Before him was his world standing right in front of him. All that truly mattered to him. He turned around and hugged and kissed his beautiful wife.

They were finally reunited, Ikedinachi could not still believe it that the day he so much longed for had come. He had dreamt of 'this day' for so long.

Similarly, Ifeoma was so delighted seeing her man although, she went mute. She admired Ikedinachi so much this time; he was the same man that she fell in love with.

She thought that England do change people, but whatever change it had done to her Ikedi is a good one.

She found him more adorable and her typical definition of a man. Ikedinachi has become more confident, loving, and caring. To her greatest amusement, Ikedinachi bought all sort of gifts for her and her little boy. They both had a suitcase to themselves.

Five years of not having Ikedinachi around that seemed like an eternity all accounted for nothing now. The feeling that encompassed her was priceless.

Ifeoma requested for an immediate leave at her workplace and it was granted. For all she cared, they had better grant it, or the next time they hear from her, she will be handing in her resignation letter. It was as though at this very moment in time, the entire world revolves around her.

They all travelled to the east to see their loved ones. In Enugu, Mr. and Mrs. Okoro were so proud of who their son has become; they celebrated his homecoming. He equally got some gift items for his parents and siblings.

Adanna was so fond of Junior and would play with him most of the time; which meant more quality time for Ikedinachi and Ifeoma.

Ikedinachi's news spread so quickly. There were numerous guests to tend to, as they came around to see Ikedinachi-the-Londoner.

Mr. Okoro was very proud of the man his son has become.

"The whiteman's country has favoured our son," he said to his wife who was in total agreement with him.

"You are right, Nkem. May the God of our ancestors continue to guide his footsteps!"

Obinna visited home from Port Harcourt and went to see his friend as soon as he could. They shared life experiences. Obinna had gotten married and has a daughter. They were both doing well for themselves.

Ikedinachi and his family visited Mr. Ugwu's family in Owerre. Ifeoma's parents were so happy to see him after all these years. They could tell already how overjoyed their daughter was as her smile wouldn't fade for a second.

Mrs. Ugwu asked that her grandson sits beside her. Ifeoma happily updated her parents and siblings about her latest travelling news, not missing out any bit. They were truly happy for her that she was finally joining her husband abroad.

Mr. Ugwu was pleased with the actions of his son-inlaw, who decided to do the right thing by coming back for his family. He advised her daughter to be careful while abroad and to always contact them especially in times of difficulty.

Mrs. Ugwu gave her daughter a motherly piece of advice, letting her know that living abroad is a good thing but can be very dangerous when certain precautions are not taken. She told her to respect her husband always, and should not be carried away by the western cultures.

As far as Mr. and Mrs. Ugwu were concerned, they have prepared their daughter for the trip to abroad.

In Enugu, Mrs. Okoro organised a thanksgiving mass for his son and his family. At the church, it was Fr. Ugoh again. He was the celebrant on their wedding day. He delivered a lovely sermon; this time he talked about love and perseverance in marriage.

At home, they incorporated send forth party for Ifeoma and Junior. All roads in Achafu street led to Ikedinachi's compound. Neighbours and friends were keen to see Ikedinachi-the-Londoner.

By evening, they were all exhausted.

Ikedinachi's mother encouraged Ifeoma to remain an obedient and hardworking wife to his son and that they should take good care of one another. She encouraged her to remember always that people are looking up to them back home.

The next day, Ikedinachi and his family travelled back to Lagos. Ifeoma handed in her resignation letter at her workplace.

Cassandra was so happy for her friend. She thought Ifeoma deserved the best.

"I will miss having you around, but I know it's for the best."

"I don't know how I would have managed well all these years without you; I will miss you too," Ifeoma replied.

Cassandra and her husband saw them off to the airport. They had snacks and drinks together. It ended up being a nice time as Ikedinachi got to meet Cassandra's husband. Most importantly, he was able to thank them for being there for his wife especially when she was pregnant.

They said their goodbyes; the two friends seemed inseparable. Cassandra kissed Junior goodbye.

"Ifeoma write to me often and tell me about England as soon as you can."

"I will."

Ikedinachi found her wife and her friend amusing. They checked in and boarded to embark on the long-awaited and dreamt journey. Junior was very playful and would not settle easily. When he eventually did, he slept. Ifeoma was curled around Ikedinachi like a baby.

"How do you feel, Darling?" Ikedinachi asked Ifeoma.

"I am so pleased to have you right here, beside me," as she talked, she ran fingers through his face; from one cheek to the other and down to his chest.

"I hope nothing separates us not even for a day. I want to be in your arms forever, Ikem."

"I have waited so long for this time in my life. I will make up for the seconds we were apart. We have our lovely world ahead of us," Ikedinachi reassured her.

"Ikem, all I can see is unalloyed happiness at last."

# Reviews

"Happiness at Last" is the first book by young Nigerian writer Vivien Ayinotu. It is a charming short story about friendship and the first steps that the characters take on leaving the security of home life. Their doubts concerning work, love and marriage are clearly and gently described. One also learns something about Nigerian traditions. An enjoyable read.

*-Peter Perring*

*Happiness at Last*
**Vivien Ayinotu**
**Author House (2017)**
**A brief review**

This novel, by a talented young author, is an important contribution to inter-cultural literature. Set in Nigeria and the UK, it is written in a style that reflects both cultures. It is the story of a relationship and marriage between to young people from Nigeria who come to the UK. Most of the book is set in Nigeria and gives the reader a rich picture of ordinary life for young people and their families. Vivien Ayinotu has much to offer to readers in different parts of the world.

*-Richard Zipfel*

Printed in Great Britain
by Amazon